CAPITOL CRIMES

2017 ANTHOLOGY

D1738987

CAPITOL CRIMES, SACRAMENTO CHAPTER OF
SISTERS IN CRIME

EDITED BY LOURDES VENARD
PROOFREAD BY FAYE ROBERTS

CAPITOL CRIMES 2017 ANTHOLOGY

Copyright 2016

Edited by Lourdes Venard

DEDICATION

Dedicated to Terri Judd, our warm and witty friend, Capitol Crimes member and short story writer. November 10, 1936-August 17, 2016.

CONTENTS

FOREWORD

By Michele Drier

Welcome to Capitol Crimes, the Sacramento chapter of Sisters in Crime. If this is your first meeting with us, we are pleased to introduce you to our national organization and to the fine local writers who could be your friends and neighbors.

The mission of Sisters in Crime is to promote the ongoing advancement, recognition and professional development of women mystery writers. Founded thirty years ago by a brave but committed band of women writers, including such well-known names as Sara Paretsky and Nancy Pickard, Sisters in Crime has grown into an international forum with chapters all over the United States and in many other countries. We now have brothers as well as sisters, and membership is open to anyone with an interest in female mystery writers: agents, editors, publishers, booksellers, librarians, and readers—most of all readers. Sisters in Crime monitors the mystery book business from publishing trends to reviews and awards and is a valued member of the mystery community.

Our local chapter started twenty years ago and serves a diverse membership through informative meetings and workshops. We consider our anthologies a learning tool for beginning writers and a showcase for our talent, whether previously published or not. And what a pool of talent we have! These fifteen stories tell of envy, revenge, blackmail, and murder in and around California's capital—and even in the Capitol itself!

Whether it's the building or the city, the capital of California captures the minds of those of us who live here. If you're a mystery writer or reader, the possibilities for mayhem are endless. We hope you will make a cup of cocoa or pour a glass of wine, curl up and be entertained.

If you would like to know more about us, visit our website: www.capitolcrimes.org or for national information see: www.sistersincrime.org.

Michele Drier was born in Santa Cruz and is a fifth generation Californian. She's lived and worked all over the state, calling both Southern and Northern California home. During her career in journalism—as a reporter and editor at daily newspapers—she won awards for producing investigative series. Her books include the Amy Hobbes Newspaper Mysteries and The Kandesky Vampire Chronicles, a paranormal romance series. She is the president of Capitol Crimes, the Sacramento chapter of Sisters in Crime.

TROUBLE WITH A CAPITAL T

KATHLEEN L. ASAY

The young woman idled among the roses in Sacramento's Capitol Park as though with no purpose, no destination, before settling down on the same bench she'd sat on yesterday and the day before. She crossed her legs—nice, slim legs Topher had noticed the first time—opened a blue cloth bag, and removed a sandwich and a bottle of water. Same sort of sandwich, same brand of water. Same pink sweater as day one but worn this time over a simple white blouse and narrow gray skirt. She had delicate features and gently curling nut-brown hair. He admired the whole package.

Topher, allowing himself a second, slow stroll past her, thought she must work in the Capitol and was possibly a new hire who hadn't yet made friends that she could join for lunch. She looked slightly uneasy on the bench, like she wasn't accustomed to eating in the park or by herself. She gazed anxiously at the people passing by and at him especially, a man of average height and indeterminate age whose own slim body and now sunken chest were hidden beneath ill-fitting clothes that looked like they'd been slept in because they had. Moreover, his black hair and beard had not been trimmed in months, and his sun-darkened skin had aged him. He understood her desire that he not come near. Still, as she had each day, she looked at him as he approached, then diverted her gaze to her lap, her lunch, before their eyes could meet.

Topher continued on to 15th Street, looked back at the Capitol dome, and sighed. He'd never expected to end up on the street. Always more an artist than a student, he'd dropped out of college his senior year when the city chose him to paint a mural on a freeway underpass near the soup kitchen where the homeless hung out. Brush in hand, he'd realized his calling: to paint thick swaths of primary colors on canvases as big as the walls where they might hang. Or to paint directly on the walls of the room, or better yet, on the outer walls of the buildings themselves. A restaurant in Midtown asked for local scenes if he could do them—just a hint of the city, the Tower Bridge, or the Capitol? Topher could and did. His signature T, as flamboyant as his art, gradually became familiar, collectible.

He even bought a small house in East Sacramento. He bought clothes. On occasion, he visited his parents so they could see he wasn't starving. He wasn't doing as well as his brother, the lawyer, but no one had expected Topher to practice law.

The fact of the matter was that Topher was a thief. In his teens, he'd taken a bully's distinctive coyote tail keychain and slipped it into the math teacher's desk drawer. The ensuing pandemonium when the teacher overreacted had been a satisfying payback to a kid who'd teased him, calling him "Toe-*fur*" because he was slight and easily picked on. Unfortunately, though the thieving was never about the loot—he'd often found a way to return it or to put it to better use— the rush of the quick grab-and-escape had proven hard to give up. When the thefts continued despite his rising career, he'd stopped visiting his parents rather than admit the jobs and friends he'd lost. After leaning on his brother Bob once or twice for legal help— all right, on three occasions—Topher no longer visited him, either.

Which, in the end, was why Topher-with-the-brilliant-T ended up homeless on the streets of Sacramento. Feeling that arrest was imminent, he'd made a short drive in the dead of night, his van full with the tools of his trade, a few clothes, and a gnome he'd always disliked that he liberated from his neighbors' wall. He left his house to his brother's care (Bob's good name was on the deed) and vanished without a word to anyone else.

Almost a year now. It was spring, late March, and his brother had taken the van and the gnome back to the house and wall, and Topher's art supplies had been reduced to what he could carry—but so had his ambitions. Colored pencil on a scrap of paper was enough to produce a portrait of the man in line for a meal or the woman serving the soup. Topher wasn't unhappy, lonely, or unfulfilled. Except maybe a little.

As the days warmed, he walked the streets from one park to another, McKinley, Cesar Chavez, Capitol. He particularly liked Capitol Park. He knew he stood out as homeless among the tourists and the business-dressed men and women who walked by without noticing the blossoms, only noticing *him*. As soon as they did, they walked a little faster, as he walked a little faster when he spotted a cop who might question what he was doing there. But he liked the atmosphere. He might be a thief, but he wasn't a hardened criminal. He'd never broken into homes or cars, or carried a weapon and threatened people. He approved of government. He admired its trappings. He admired the woman in the park. It had been a long while since anything like *that* had happened.

He slowly circled back to where she still ate her lunch on the park bench, staring ahead at the roses, or at nothing. Her purse sat behind her right elbow, open. Topher approached from the left and leaned down.

"Looks like a good sandwich," he said.

She looked up, startled, and pulled the sandwich close as though to protect it from him. Her eyes were wide meeting his. Dark blue. Nice eyes but the eyes of a person who was troubled by more than the unwanted attention of a street person. Topher stared into them while his hand slipped into her purse.

"Sorry," he said. "I didn't mean anything. Just—you make your own sandwiches?"

She retreated until her back was against the back of the bench. He saw realization strike her when she could go no further. Immediately, she began to wrap up her meal and feel for her handbag.

He stepped back so she could stand. She wasn't tall; he had a head on her.

"You don't have to go," he said in a rush. "I will. I'm sorry."

7

"I'm going," she said. Firm. She turned away, toward the Capitol.

Topher gave her fifty feet before he pulled her wallet from his pocket. He flipped it open and read her driver's license. Trotted after her.

When he was within fifteen feet, he said, "Gwendolyn."

She stopped and looked at him over her shoulder.

"You dropped this," he said.

Her eyes went to the tan leather in his hand, then widened on him. "You stole my wallet."

He shrugged, came closer, and held it out. She grabbed it from him and quickly checked through it while Topher watched.

"I just wanted to know your name," he said. "I'm not a bad person."

"You're a thief."

Said like that, he wished it weren't true. He lowered his head, nodded.

"I'm going." She took a step away.

"Come tomorrow?"

She squared her shoulders and strode on, did not look back.

Gwen. He smiled. Whistled.

He made good use of the next twenty-three hours: showered, cut his nails, trimmed his hair and his beard but didn't shave (he'd been told facial hair was in fashion), and in the morning, he dressed in his few clean clothes. He considered going home for better clothes and nicer-smelling soap, but he'd have to break in and he was afraid to take a chance.

It didn't matter anyway because she didn't come. He sat on the bench with his hands between his knees and felt worse than he had in over a year. After a while, a family of tourists came by, two middle-schoolers and their parents talking about lunch, and the conversation clicked in Topher's mind. Tourists— kids—no school—Saturday! Topher grinned at the straggler kid.

He'd only been watching the wrong direction, anyway. "I brought you a sandwich," Gwen said. "And water. That's all I had. Sorry I'm late. I had to park a few blocks from here."

She sounded breathless, still nervous. In honor of Saturday and the heat, she wore a T-shirt, capris, and sandals. She'd pulled her hair back. He took it all in, liking what he saw.

"I almost didn't recognize you," she said. "You're"—she gestured at him from top to bottom—"different."

"Different clothes," he agreed. "And I got my hair cut."

"You're sitting on my bench."

"Oh, sorry."

He scrambled to his feet, but she gestured him back down. "Just sit at that end."

He grinned and sat, watched her settle herself at the other end, three feet and a sandwich between them. She held the food out to him.

"You know my name. What's yours?"

"Topher—Christopher, but my dad is Chris, so they call me Topher."

"Oh. Eat. I hope you like egg salad."

"Love it." He took a bite. The bread was fresh, chewy; egg and mayo slipped out between his fingers. When he licked them, she handed him a pile of napkins.

After he'd eaten the first half, he said, "Something's troubling you, and it's not me. I don't think the hardware I felt in your purse is meant for me. You have a license for it?"

"Oh!" She lifted her handbag like she was about to leave. "I knew this was a mistake."

"No," he said quickly, "it's not a mistake. Maybe I can help."

"*You*? How?"

"Do you know anything about guns?"

She withered under his probing eyes. "I know you can make a mess of yourself with one if you try."

He stretched a hand out toward her on the bench, said, "I'm sorry." Waited.

"My little sister meant to kill herself," she said, "but she missed. She'd have been better off if she'd succeeded." She gazed down at her lap, then back at his face. "Have you heard of an assemblyman named Buckley? He's from down the Valley. My sister campaigned for him in his first race two years ago, and he offered her a job in his office here in Sacramento. She knew he liked to hit on the women in his office, but he'd never bothered her so she took the job. Then this September somebody recorded him and some other legislators in a bar talking. Buckley was saying how he had an aide who did great work, which was good because she—she—because the governor's dog was more attractive."

"Your sister?" he asked in a low voice.

"It went viral, but it didn't stop him being reelected in November. Two weeks later, she tried to kill herself. She hit the side of her head when she'd intended to shoot her ugly face."

He closed his eyes, feeling sick. He wanted to touch her hand and offer comfort, but instead he gestured toward her purse. "And the gun?"

She hoisted her chin. "He won't be reelected again."

"You can't do that."

"Why not? You're going to stop me? You're a thief."

"Yeah, and I'm living on the street because I'd rather do that than go to jail. Do you think the cops are going to let you shoot him and walk away? Your sister is still alive. What will she think if you're in jail or dead?"

"She won't know!" She shuddered and tears came, a deluge.

Topher passed her the remaining napkins. He took a bite of the second half of his sandwich. After a few minutes, the sandwich was nearly gone, and Gwen's tears had been reduced to sniffles.

"How can you *eat*?" she asked.

"I'm hungry."

She watched him swallow the last crust.

"How old are you?"

"Twenty-nine," he said. "How old are you?"

"Thirty."

"Oh. I thought you were younger."

She blushed. "I thought you were older. If you're twenty-nine, you should have a job. Have you *ever* had a job?"

"Sure. I paint. But a year ago, when I painted a restaurant, I got into the boss's wife's purse for a five to give a homeless guy who was hanging around. 'Cause I didn't carry cash. She caught me. Her husband laughed it off, but she pressed charges and let it be known around that I couldn't be trusted."

"Oh."

"I'm a thief, but I don't touch guns. You shouldn't either."

"That's my business!"

"Well, how are you going to get it into the Capitol?"

"I don't plan to. I keep it in my car. I'm going to shoot him out here. He walks in the park when he doesn't want anyone to overhear his conversation, so he's out here often." She shook her head in disgust. "Anyway, I'm not going to kill him. I'll just nick him between the legs."

Topher nearly choked on the laugh that bubbled up. "Sure you will, Annie Oakley. You're more likely to shoot yourself between the legs."

"I can aim it," she argued. "I've been practicing. You have a better idea?"

"No, but—what's he look like?"

He was not surprised to see her dig into her purse. He rose, walked to nearby shrubs, pulled out his carryall, and brought it back to the bench. It took him a minute to find his sketchbook and a drawing pencil. Gwen's eyes were wide when she handed over a newspaper clipping.

"That's him, in the middle."

Topher frowned. He'd seen the man, seen him seek a private spot for a confab with another man or maybe two, seen him talk on the phone. He was given to decisive language and harsh gestures. Point made, he'd swagger toward the Capitol.

"Your sister picked a good one."

"He's good-looking, and he says the right things."

"I'll bet." Topher thought for a moment, then began to draw. Quick strokes, he still liked broad lines and impressions more than photo accuracy. He handed the sketchbook to her when he was done.

She squealed. "Oh, my God, that's him! That's—it's amazing. You said you paint, but *this* is what you do?"

"Well, usually with the subject's approval."

"Oh, I wish my sister could see this. That looks just like the governor's dog. And Buckley chasing it with his pants down. Oh, I think I'm going to cry."

"Please, no more."

"If you can do this, why aren't you doing it?"

"Do I have to remind you?"

"But—"

"You don't really work in the Capitol, do you?"

"What? Of course, I do. Why do you ask?"

"It just came to me. You sitting here for three days, and coming back today, talking to me. You don't look like the sort who would tell her troubles to a homeless person. I'm thinking Bob sent you. You went to him first, and when he couldn't help you, he sent you to me, told you my name."

She looked genuinely perplexed. "Who's Bob?"

Topher didn't know whether to be angry or to believe her. "My brother. He's a lawyer in town. It'd be just like him to think if I help you, I'll get recognized and sent to jail, and jail will cure me. No more stealing. You're the perfect bait, a woman with a problem. Is the problem real?"

"*Yes*. But I don't know Bob, I promise. I just—"

"You just picked me?"

She gathered up her purse like she might run, then collapsed, defeated. "Please," she said. "I felt sorry for you when you asked about my sandwich. I thought I'd bring you one. That's all. I wasn't going to talk to you. I just … did."

She took a deep breath, drew it out. "If you must know, I teach school, fourth grade. I took the semester off as compassionate leave. My kids should be studying California history about now." She tossed her head to stop the insistent tears, sniffles. "I got a job down the hall from Buckley for the spring and summer, 'til I can get this done. I see him around, talking, flirting. Then I visit my sister in the nursing home. That's my incentive."

"To shoot the bastard."

"Right."

"I won't help you. In fact, if I were on better terms with the police, I'd turn you in. Save you from yourself. The drawing is yours. Do what you want with it. I'd just like my sketchbook back."

"Topher—" Her eyes pleaded with him, but for what? Understanding? She held the book out. "Please. I don't want it."

He stood, took the sketchbook from her and ripped out the page with the drawing, threw it down. It floated to the bench where he'd been sitting. Topher stuffed the book and pencil back into his bag, draped the bag over his shoulder, and walked to L Street. When he looked back, she was gone. The drawing lay on the bench. It rose slightly in the breeze. He hurried back to catch it.

***

He should have taken the gun. The thought pressed on him. For a man with endless time on his hands, he suddenly felt a need to hurry. He spent a restless night. Sunday, he washed his face in a Starbucks restroom a block from Macy's, and he buried his pack in the coffeehouse's shrubbery. He didn't like to leave it, but he couldn't risk taking it into the department store and being asked to leave because he looked homeless or, ironically, like a thief. Starbucks had been safe before; he would just have to chance it.

On the ground floor of Macy's, he found what he was looking for when a well-dressed woman made a purchase in the handbag department. He brushed by her, apologized, and kept going. In a quiet corner, he extracted a twenty and three ones from her wallet and silently apologized again. "It's for a good cause," he added.

A few minutes later, when another clerk took over the handbag counter, he approached, bent down, then stood up and held out the wallet.

"Someone dropped this," he said. He even accepted a minute of profuse thanks.

With cash in his pocket, he mapped out his activities for the next day. He needed an office supply store and a copy machine, and he had to visit the Capitol Annex where Gwen and Buckley worked, as well as the post office. Meanwhile, he'd do a wash; he wanted to be wearing clean clothes when the cops picked him up. He pulled out the drawing of Buckley and boldly scrawled his trademark T at the bottom.

***

She didn't shoot him, not Monday, not Tuesday. Topher hung around the park each day, saw the assemblyman chat with others, didn't see Gwen at all. He tried to catch the evening news on television. Each night, he breathed a sigh of relief. If his presence in the park was a deterrent, he'd be there every day.

On Friday, a nurse who often visited the shelter called Topher aside and held out a sheet of paper. It was a photocopy of his drawing.

"Did you do this?" she asked. "They're saying you did. On the news."

Topher closed his eyes. Nodded. Finally. His eyes opened wide when she spoke again.

"Did you know the women in Assemblyman Buckley's office have been protesting their boss?" she asked. "They're circulating this drawing and a flyer talking about the woman he humiliated six months ago. She tried to kill herself. Now other women are speaking up. Can you believe it? He'd been looking like a shoo-in for the next speaker, and now he'll have to resign his office!" She laughed, clearly pleased. "How did you get involved?"

"I—a woman." He paused, found nothing to say. "I didn't know—" He gestured at the drawing.

"You're famous." She gave his shoulders a squeeze. "But we won't tell on you."

14

Topher arranged to watch the news on TV that night. Assemblyman Rowan Buckley issued a brief statement that while he did not feel he had harmed anyone, apparently some staffers did. He was bowing to their request that he resign his office. His family looked forward to having him home more.

Reporters followed with word that the campaign by Buckley's staffers and others in the Assembly offices had been inspired by a drawing that came in the mail to many of the women. They didn't know who had sent it—it had a return address for a Starbucks in town, but local artists had identified the signature on the sketch as belonging to Topher Hall. Topher was well known in the art community, though no one had seen him for many months. The press had yet to obtain a photograph of him, but they gave his description along with the information that there was an arrest warrant out for him for theft. The female reporter speculated that if Topher would come forward, the charges were likely to be dropped in light of the current favorable publicity.

Topher remained in his chair long after the broadcast ended. As the shelter began to bed down for the night, he let himself out into the mild evening darkness and began to walk. He didn't hurry; the sky was brightening when he reached his destination.

The cheeky gnome laughed at him from atop his neighbors' wall. Topher walked around to his own backyard, stretched out on a lawn chair, and slept.

***

An irritated judge gave Topher a lecture but ordered community service rather than waste jail space. Two days a week, Topher taught art in a community center that served the poor and mentally ill. The rest of the week, he painted in pencil. In September, eight new works in a series Topher called "Street Scenes—Sacramento," featuring the faces of the homeless he'd met, the prone figures on the sidewalks, and the illegal tent cities, were included in a show at a Midtown art gallery. The show opened for Second Saturday gallery night. Wine was served. Friends and family of the artists crowded the small space.

Topher, clean-shaven and with his hair trimmed so it only curled over his collar, stood alone late in the evening after saying goodbye to his family, who had been among the first in the door. A voice he had not expected to hear again spoke from beside him.

"Are you done with thieving?" Gwen asked.

"Not quite," he admitted, barely daring to look at her. "I have one more heist in mind."

"Oh?"

"I'm planning to steal you away from here. Do you think anyone will mind?"

She made a show of scanning the room. Smiled at last. "They might, but if you're quick, they may not notice."

Kathleen L. Asay, a lifelong writer and editor, has been a member of three chapters of Sisters in Crime and is a former president of Capitol Crimes. She had stories in and edited Capitol Crimes' two previous anthologies. Her first novel, *Flint House* (BridlePath Press, 2013), features a run-down Sacramento boarding house, a burned out journalist and a mysterious older woman whose story might save them all. Visit Kathleen at www.KathleenLAsay.com.

AGNES WINS AGAIN

ELAINE FABER

Agnes pushed a tiny metal basket through the aisle of Wilkey's Market. *Coffee ... coffee ...* She glanced at the single red stamp still clinging to the binding of her War Ration Stamps book. Since the Japanese invasion of Manila, coffee and sugar were nearly impossible to bring onto the mainland. She supposed that rationing was necessary, but only one pound of coffee every six weeks per adult? Wasn't cruel and unusual punishment banned by the Constitution or the Bill of Rights, or something? Thank goodness, with her granddaughter, Katherine, living with her, they could purchase two pounds every six weeks. *Ooh, wouldn't I like to wring the scrawny neck of whoever in the White House makes me suffer so.*

As she approached the coffee section, the delightful aroma of freshly ground coffee beans created a symphony in her mouth. Next to the large red grinder sat a glass bin full of dark brown beans. She moved the silver scoop under the spout and pulled the lever. Beans tumbled out. She shoved the lever back, dumped the beans into the top of the coffee grinder, and cranked the side handle.

Miniscule grains of ground coffee spilled out like chocolate sand. Agnes carefully held a brown paper bag beneath the spout, lest she lose even a grain, and imagined fresh ground coffee tomorrow morning. The bouquet of coffee beans rose from the bag Agnes clutched in her hand.

The ground coffee bag tipped the scales at just under a pound. At seventy-four cents a pound, that would cost just about seventy cents! Incredible! Price gouging! *My! What we have to pay to indulge our guilty pleasures.*

Since all the best meat went to the troops, buying a decent cut was even worse. Not that she begrudged the troops. Didn't she knit socks, collect papers and cans, serve on the coast watch, and volunteer at the USO? Always first to volunteer for any worthy cause to help the war effort, she accepted the challenges as a warrior on the home front. But somebody needed to do something about the unreasonable rationing of her coffee. *Why not me?* Maybe she could convince Katherine to take a few days off work at the beauty shop and come with her.

They could go to Sacramento and speak to the governor. If he heard directly from a couple of homemakers, perhaps he could ease some of the burdens of rationing, at least on her coffee.

***

Dear Governor Olson:

You don't know me, but my granddaughter, Katherine, and I are taking the bus all the way to Sacramento next Friday to speak with you about a disturbing situation right here in Newbury.

I'm sure you are very busy running California, but we feel we must bring this matter of vital concern to your attention in hopes you can help. We believe someone of your importance will have the influence to change this dreadful situation.

Sincerely, Agnes Agatha Odboddy

Agnes sealed up the letter, mailed it, and called the bus station to reserve tickets to Sacramento the following Friday. Some matters can be addressed through the mail, but sometimes you just have to present important issues in person. The authorities might ignore a written request, but it would be harder for the governor to justify continuing an unreasonable situation when you're presenting it face to face.

***

"Arriving from Santa Rosa, 11:45 a.m. Departing to Sacramento, 12:20 p.m." The hubbub of voices in the bus station nearly drowned out the announcement on the loudspeaker.

The bus station rumbled with mixed human emotions that ran the gamut from joy to sorrow, from exuberant hello hugs to tearful, clinging goodbye kisses.

Agnes checked her tickets. "We have a few minutes before our connecting bus leaves for Sacramento. Let's find a seat and eat our lunch." She picked up her suitcase and steered Katherine to a quieter section of the station, where she plopped onto a wooden bench. Agnes rummaged in her purse and pulled out two liverwurst sandwiches, carrot sticks, and several crumpled oatmeal cookies. "We'd best eat before we get on board. I hear that food prices in Sacramento are high. After we see Governor Olson, I want to tour the Capitol building and visit the shops in downtown Sacramento. We mustn't waste our money on food. Carrot stick?"

Katherine took the carrot. "Always the prime objective! Save money," she mumbled as she snapped off a bite of carrot.

The crowd rushed hither and yon. Soldiers bought tickets, women wept, girls threw themselves into soldiers' arms, and babies shrieked.

Agnes shook her head. "It just breaks my heart. So many young men going off to—"

Her bench squeaked as a man in a rumpled coat plopped down beside her. He turned a weary face toward her and mumbled, "Morning."

"Morning." Agnes nodded. She munched her sandwich as she sized him up. *Farmer? Refugee? Unemployed? Hasn't shaved for several days. Needs a bath.* She held out the crumpled cookie. "Would you care for a cookie?"

Tears sprang to the man's eyes. He put his hand over his face and shook his head. "My wife used to bake oatmeal cookies for my son. When he died of smallpox somewhere in the Pacific Islands, I contacted the governor to see if they'd send his body home. He never even answered my letter." He lowered his voice, as though he were thinking out loud. "He can't treat folks this way and live to tell about it."

Agnes coughed. "You mean Governor Olson, in Sacramento? We're on our way to see him now." She fidgeted on the bench and caught Katherine's eye.

Katherine jerked her head, clearly suggesting they move on.

Agnes shook her head. "Just a minute, Katherine. Mister, you don't look so well. Do you need some help? I could call someone for you."

The man looked up, his eyes still sparkling with tears. "I can take care of myself. Never needed no help before. Don't need any now." He patted his coat pocket and squared his jaw. His eyes took on a steely sheen as he glared at the American flag on a nearby wall. "Government for the people ... *bah!*"

Agnes shivered, grabbed her purse and pulled out her bus ticket. She leaned toward Katherine and raised her voice to be heard over the drone in the great room. "Our bus leaves for Sacramento in a few minutes." She glanced at her watch. "We'd best be on our way!"

Agnes grabbed her suitcase and hustled Katherine toward the ladies' room.

"That was weird!" Katherine nodded back toward the bench.

A porter rushed by with a pushcart filled with luggage.

"Sir! Sir! Excuse me. Can you take our suitcases to the Sacramento bus?" Agnes held out her suitcase and nodded to the one Katherine carried.

"Sure can, ma'am. I'm heading that way with this load now." The porter stacked their suitcases on top of his trolley.

"That's most kind of you." Agnes reached into her purse and handed him a dime.

"Thank you, ma'am. Much obliged." He rushed off toward the exit with his load.

Katherine clutched her grandmother's arm. "Grandma. Do you think that man on the bench means to hurt Governor Olson? He looked so angry. He scared me."

"Don't worry, punkin. Lots of folks are hurting these days. He probably just lost his son in the war. People say all kinds of things when they're hurting. They don't mean anything by it."

"But did you see the way he patted his pocket? Do you think he had a gun?" Katherine shivered. "Maybe we should tell someone. They say we're supposed to report anything suspicious."

"Don't be silly. The poor man has enough problems without being hauled into the police station for popping off something stupid in a bus station. Besides, he didn't actually threaten the governor. He could have meant anything by what he said."

"I suppose you're right." Katherine cast a worried glance toward the man as he turned and stalked off toward the buses.

Agnes pushed her way through a long line of ladies waiting outside the restroom, where patriotic posters hung on the wall over the door. LOOSE LIPS SINK SHIPS. BUY AMERICAN WAR BONDS.

"Excuse me. Pardon me. Can you let us through here, please?"

A large, blonde woman with a ruddy complexion held up her hand. "Hey! Pardon yourself, lady. We've been waiting for nearly ten minutes already!"

"Then I'm sure you wouldn't mind if we cut in front of you?" Agnes flashed her most charming smile and nodded, while mentally measuring the distance between the restroom door and her ability to wait in the long line for the restroom. "You don't understand," she said, adjusting the chopsticks in her bun, "we have a bus to catch in a couple minutes."

"As a matter of fact, I do mind. We all have a bus to catch. Who do you think you are? Some kind of celebrity?" The line moved forward a few feet as a woman exited the swinging door.

Agnes turned toward Katherine. "Guess she doesn't know about our important business in Sacramento."

"Grandma! *Hush!*" Katherine's face flushed as she turned her back on her grandmother.

The woman in line glared at Agnes.

Agnes glared back. "That's right, Blondie. For your information, we have official business at the State Capitol. What's your name? If we don't make the bus, Governor Culbert Olson will want to know which unpatriotic upstart made us miss our appointment." She reached into her purse, as if to pull out a pencil.

The woman started and moved back a step. She sputtered. "What? That bum? I could tell you a thing or two about that traitor, but he's not worth my time to … *Humph!*" Her cheeks flamed. She blinked several times, and then lowered her head, turned, and hurried away from the restroom.

"The governor doesn't seem to be very well liked around here, does he? Oh well. Her loss is our gain." Agnes bypassed the ladies still waiting and stood at the head of the line.

"Grandma, really. You've about embarrassed me to death!"

Agnes chuckled as she entered the next empty stall, hung her jacket on the peg, hitched up her skirt, and sat. *Ahh! Oh, thank goodness! And not a second too soon.*

She glanced at the graffiti on the stall door. Why were people so rude these days? During World War I, folks were thoughtful and kind. If she'd asked someone for a favor, they'd have fallen all over themselves to oblige.

Agnes adjusted her clothing, retrieved her jacket, and stepped toward the sinks where Katherine stood, washing her hands. "Come, dear, we must hurry."

Once clear of the restroom, Katherine said, "Grandma. How could you speak to that woman like that? What's gotten into you?"

"Now, where is that Sacramento bus?"

"Don't change the subject, Grandma. You know what I'm talking about. All that malarkey about being on official business. You can't lie to folks just to get to the head of the line. I've never been so embarrassed."

Agnes stopped walking and turned in a circle, checking the signs high on the walls indicating arrival and departure times. "There. Due north." She shoved the silver chopsticks more firmly into her bun. Determined as Lewis and Clark searching for a route across the western continent, Agnes plunged through the crowd toward the waiting Sacramento bus.

Katherine's cheeks pinked up as she hurried to catch up. "Well? You have nothing to say?"

"It worked, didn't it? We would never have gotten through that line and made the bus at the rate we were going. Besides, I had to ... Never mind ... Do I need to draw you a picture?"

"Grandmother. You are a caution! Sometimes I just don't know what to do with you."

***

The Greyhound bus cruised through Sonoma County past fields of grazing cows and sheep. Through the Fairfield and Vacaville area, only scattered houses could be seen from the highway, while stalks of corn and wheat bent in the wind, soon to be turned into food for the nation and the troops overseas.

Agnes looked over her shoulder toward the back of the bus. Halfway down the aisle, the woman from the restroom frowned as Agnes caught her eye.

Warmth crept up Agnes' neck. Perhaps she had been a bit rude. *Oh, well!*

Agnes spotted the rumpled man from the bus station huddled in the very last row, his coat pulled tightly around his chest and his hands in his pockets. He stared out the windows, his jaw set, his expression determined, as though resolved to some unknown mission.

Gee willikers! Looks like the gang's all here! A chill raced up Agnes' spine. Was the man planning some harm to the governor? Had she been too quick to shrug off Katherine's suggestion to notify the authorities? She worried in silence, reluctant to share her concerns with Katherine. After all, she hadn't wanted to come along on this trip in the first place and nothing could be done about the man on the bus, anyway. Maybe she was wrong. With luck, he might disembark in Vallejo. Why jump to conclusions when all you have are unconfirmed suspicions?

***

The bus arrived in Sacramento and after securing a room at Hotel Cluny on K Street, Agnes and Katherine hailed a taxi headed for the State Capitol.

"Katherine, are you aware that the Capitol building is identical to the one in Washington, DC? See the columns in front and the round roof?"

Katherine rolled her eyes. "Yes, Grandma. I did go to college, you know. Let's get this over with! You don't even know if we can get in to see the governor."

Agnes followed Katherine up the Capitol steps and through the double doors. Two uniformed soldiers stood guard at the entry. "Time to make nice and charm the gentlemen, Katherine," Agnes whispered.

Katherine nodded and approached the soldier. "Excuse me. Can you direct us to the governor's office?" Katherine's bewitching smile could melt the ears off a chocolate Easter bunny. "We're hoping to get a few minutes with him today."

One soldier blushed, stammered, and pointed to the elevator. "Second floor, third door to the left, but I doubt you can get in without an appointment. You may have to come back tomorrow."

"Oh, dear. I do hope not. We've come so far. Wish us luck." Another enchanting grin and the soldier's blush crept further up his neck.

Across the lobby, the rumpled man from the bus leaned against the wall by the water fountain.

Agnes turned back to the soldier and whispered, "See that man over there by the fountain? We heard him at the bus station, saying some odd things. Sounded like he was referring to the governor."

"Like threats, ma'am?" The soldier's hand flew to this holster.

"Not exactly threats, but if I were you I'd keep an eye on him."

Katherine looked back over her shoulder as Agnes hauled her toward the elevators. The man by the fountain had moved on down the hall and one of the soldiers followed close behind.

When they reached the governor's office, Agnes and Katherine greeted the secretary sitting outside the door. "We'd like to see Governor Olson, please." Agnes grinned. Her smile did not have the same effect on the secretary as Katherine's had on the soldier.

The secretary scowled and checked her schedule book. "He's very busy today. I'm afraid an appointment is quite impossible." She flipped forward a page. "Maybe tomorrow?"

"Oh, can't you squeeze us in for just a couple minutes? We've been on the bus for four hours and our business is quite important."

"Well, perhaps he can see you for just a few minutes." The secretary poked her head in the door and inquired. "Governor Olson says he can see you right now, if you make it quick." She ushered them into his office.

"Have a seat, ladies. What's on your mind?" The governor lit a cigarette and gestured to two chairs in front of his desk.

"Thank you for seeing us, sir." Agnes sat and placed her purse on the floor. "I'm Agnes Odboddy and this is my granddaughter, Katherine. We came all the way from Newbury to discuss an unreasonable rationing situation. How does the government expect a person to survive on only one pound of coffee every six weeks? It's downright—"

At that moment, the door opened and slammed against the wall. The woman from the bus station restroom burst into the room, shoving the secretary ahead of her, a .32-caliber Colt pistol pointed toward her head. "Hold it right there, Governor!"

Agnes leaped from her chair. She took a step toward the woman. *My stars! It's Blondie, from the bus station bathroom!*

The woman's gun hand wavered when she saw Agnes standing in front of the governor's desk. "You! What on earth are you doing in here?"

Agnes' hand moved to the back of her head as though adjusting her bun. "I could ask you the same. I told you, back in

27

Santa Rosa, we had an important meeting with the governor. You never mentioned you were headed to the Capitol with murder on your mind. What's your beef?" *Holy Moly! A body isn't safe anywhere these days with crazed killers behind every rock.*

The woman sneered. "Thanks to Governor Olson's new tax plan, I've lost my farm and my life savings!" The woman's voice shook with emotion. "There's nothing left for me. Now, it's your turn, Governor. You're going to pay with your life!" She aimed the pistol toward him.

"Jumping Jehoshaphat, lady! Have you lost your mind?" The governor jumped up.

Agnes took another step closer. "Hold it right there, Blondie. Let's take a moment and think about this. We've been sitting on a bus for four straight hours, and my rump aches like thunder, just so I could present my problem to an official representative of the government."

Agnes advanced another step toward the woman. She reached out a hand. "I understand why you'd be upset with losing your farm like that, and I sympathize, but you've got to see things my way, too. Here I am discussing an important issue with the governor, only to be interrupted by someone intent on murder. It's quite exasperating, to say the least. What do you say? As serious as I'm sure you feel your grievance is, do you mind coming back after lunch to commit murder?"

"Grandma! What are you saying? You're rationalizing with the woman about the timing of her murder plot?"

A bewildered expression crossed the woman's face as she gazed from Katherine to the governor and back to Agnes.

"Quite right, my dear!" Governor Olson added. "Another time would be much more appropriate, say, when my security guard is present!" He moved behind his desk.

Blondie's lips trembled. She wrinkled her forehead as though she were trying to process Agnes' and the governor's nonsensical requests. Her gun hand trembled as she lowered it a few inches.

The secretary, apparently seeing an unexpected opportunity to escape, made a break for the door, flung it open, and disappeared, shrieking, into the hallway.

As the assailant turned the gun toward her escaping hostage, the governor crouched behind his desk.

Agnes yanked a silver chopstick from her hair, rushed forward, and jabbed it into the woman's shoulder.

Blondie jerked back. A shot rang out and a bullet slammed into the governor's desk just above his cowering head. The pistol tumbled to the floor. She screamed in pain and tried to escape just as a marine, responding to the commotion, rushed in.

The two grappled and no sooner than it takes to say "Jack Robinson," the would-be assassin lay crumpled on the carpet, moaning and clutching her shoulder.

Governor Olson popped up from behind his desk. His hand trembled as he reached for the cigarette that lay burning in his ashtray. "*Ahem* ... Good work, *umm* ... Mrs. Ombraditty."

"Odboddy! Agnes Odboddy!" Agnes snapped.

"Of course! Of course! I was just about to rush the perpetrator myself when you beat me to the punch. *Heh! Heh!* How can I ever thank you, Mrs. Ombidotty? Perhaps you and your lovely granddaughter will stay for lunch? We can discuss your concerns over tuna fish sandwiches. I believe we can even rustle up a few White House cookies."

The culprit's wails reverberated down the hall as the marine hauled her out the door.

Katherine clutched her grandmother's arm. "Grandma! Whatever got into you? You scared me half to death. You could have been killed."

Agnes patted Katherine's arm. "There, there now. Didn't we come all this way to discuss our coffee rations with the governor? I couldn't let that crazy woman kill him. It could take *months* to elect another governor. I can't wait that long to straighten out this rationing situation." Agnes grinned, pulled out her hankie, and wiped the blood off her chopstick before shoving it back into her bun. "By the way, I think we misjudged that man we saw at the bus station. Before we leave the building, let's see if we can find him. I'd like to buy him a cup of coffee."

"Makes sense to me, Grandma. I wouldn't mind a cup myself."

Elaine Faber is a member of Sisters in Crime, Inspire Christian Writers, and Cat Writers Association. She has published three cozy cat mysteries and a WWII mystery-adventure. Elaine's short stories are included in eight anthologies and various magazines. If you enjoy *Agnes Wins Again*, follow her complete adventures in the humorous WWII novel, *Mrs. Odboddy Hometown Patriot*, available at Amazon in print and e-book.

SEEING THINGS

JUNE GILLAM

The memory care home near Land Park was as close to our old neighborhood as I could find for my sister. It wasn't bad either—the air was fresh thanks to the top-notch ventilation system, making the place more expensive than other assisted living facilities. I was grateful I could afford a private room for Terri. This morning the hallway was dotted with old people in wheelchairs, some nodding off, some mumbling to themselves. A few women were dressed in the home's pale-blue cotton gowns, their slippers and bunchy cardigans lending personal touches. I strode past them on my weekly visit to Terri. It was my duty. She had never married and I was the only family she had left.

Outside her door, I stopped and listened. She was at it again, spinning yarns from the old days, talking to that steel mirror on the wall. Glass would have been too dangerous, setting up the owners for lawsuits in case of accident. Terri no longer understood she was addressing her own image, couldn't see reality the way I did every morning when I shaved, jutting out my chin to firm up my jawline. Clear blue eyes. Close-cropped hair still only lightly dusted with gray.

California's capital city trusted me to prosecute the guilty. Never mind that a few of them slipped through now and again.

There wasn't any use correcting Terri. The stories she told were nothing like what really happened. I was a couple years older than my sister, but I had a memory like a movie camera. Always had. Always would.

We lived on Riverside back then, across the street from the Old City Cemetery in the nicest house south of Edmonds Field. Father's law firm was prospering, so he'd bought a double lot and had our house built at midpoint. It turned out looking like a

33

square white cake standing proudly in the middle of a big green lawn. On Riverside north toward Broadway was another lot, a big vacant one. Nowadays, I think it's a Chinese restaurant or something. All things get covered up with time.

Father had just been elected to Sacramento's City Council the month before we moved into the fancy house. We had finally escaped the run-down neighborhood I'd felt ashamed of. In our new surroundings, Mother let us roam free. Terri had taken to roller-skating around our huge block, her skates falling off every few houses. I'd have to get off my bike and help her fit them back onto her oxfords, tightening them down with the skate key, but the shoe and the skate combination never held for long. So I'd ride behind her on my Schwinn Hornet, at the ready. Terri's cute new friends would skate out from their driveways and join her, their short skirts blowing in the breeze. I'd let them get ahead of me and enjoy the view. Guys I met in Land Park began following along, too. I started to feel like the leader of the pack.

***

This morning, I bent down to kiss Terri on her soft, wrinkled cheek. She grinned. "I was just telling Mary, my new roommate—" She waved her black knit shawl toward the mirror on the wall. "Have you met Mary?"

I nodded silently. It was no use correcting Terri anymore.

She went on. "Telling her how Daddy built a merry-go-round for the whole neighborhood that second summer in the new house."

I nodded. That was her story. No matter that it was just a worn circle in the tall grass of the vacant lot near Broadway. The girls would trample down the weeds with their skates and clear a path they could try to glide over. It was so bumpy they would collapse in hysterical laughter, unbuckle their skates and sit cross-legged in a circle, feigning dizziness, as my friends and I parked our bikes in the tall grass back away from the street.

34

"Mary was shocked when I let her in on my secret." Terri frowned and looked away from the mirror. "It wasn't so safe in Land Park, after all."

I shook my head. How she carried on.

She sucked at her top teeth and glared at me. "Why did you and your pals desert us? Why not protect us? You were big and strong." Her story was going in a new direction. Before, Terri had blamed Mother for the attack that day, blamed her for letting her friends and her skate so far from home. Blamed a gang of guys from the wrong side of Broadway, wearing black knit ski masks. Blamed that awful attack on her being afraid of men, never marrying. She never even had a serious boyfriend.

"I've been working real hard to remember, and it came to me last night in a dream." She scowled and snatched up a piece of paper from her desk. "I wrote it down." She squinted, put on her glasses, and nodded as she scanned the paper, marked with circles and zigzagged lines. Then she turned and drew her shawl across her face, looking like an Arab woman whose eyes were the only feature showing. "Look at yourself!" Her voice was loud and strong through the loose knit of her shawl.

She stood and tottered over to me, reached up to lay her black shawl across the bottom half of my face. With boney fingers that felt like iron claws, she turned me to face the polished steel mirror on the wall. "There! There is the leader of that pack, wearing your true color. Black! All this time, you've played the good guy. Sending criminals to their just rewards. Ha! The best was the worst of all."

Frozen in place, I could see my face in the mirror. My blue eyes above a black knit mask, a match to those I'd handed out to the neighborhood guys I was trying to impress.

Terri collapsed back into her chair, sobbing, the shawl falling to the floor. I stood there staring into the mirror, tears rolling down my cheeks, the stainless steel of my reflection fracturing into a silver kaleidoscope. Each shard of the truth convicted me, a prosecutor all these years trying to get criminals sent off to prison, criminals like the ones I'd led into that assault against my sister and her friends. And then buried so deep down in my memory bank.

June Gillam's fiction explores the mind of characters whose shadow side is set free at some point to energize their criminal potential. In the Hillary Broome novels, Gillam investigates the impact of a superstore on a small town butcher in *House of Cuts,* the consequence of patriarchy on a woman in business in *House of Dads,* and the effect of a Donald-Trump type developer on Irish tourism in *House of Eire*. Details at www.junegillam.com.

COUNTING TO TEN

R. FRANKLIN JAMES

Lauren couldn't count to ten.

Sitting in the committee room, she went over the single sheet of names for the third time, and shook her head.

Just maybe she could count to eight.

Phil Mercer had been adamant that, without a majority vote of ten, their flagship public works bill would go down in flames; and more importantly, her career as a political consultant would end before it got started. He was the office's legislative guru, and hadn't wanted Assemblyman Byron Dennison to hire her from the start.

"What's wrong?" Don Eastbrook asked. He was Assemblyman Mitchell's staffer, and the opposition. "You look like you have an appointment for an overdue root canal." He eased into the empty chair next to hers and slightly leaned over, talking but looking straight ahead.

"Nothing that would interest you." She spoke in a likewise fashion, not turning to face him. It wouldn't be good to be seen chatting with the other side.

They both stiffened as the Assembly committee vote was called.

"Seven ayes and six nays. AB 1243 will move forward to the conference committee," the secretary called out.

Lauren smiled. "Sorry about that."

He frowned. "No, you're not. This gives you another notch in your job security belt." He scribbled a note on a piece of paper and put it in his shirt pocket. "But I don't think you'll be so lucky when your boss's bill is taken up."

"We're confident that the votes will be there. Besides, there's still time to maneuver."

"Oh, yeah." Don hit his temple with the palm of his hand. "Wait, I forgot to tell you. The committee chair was asked to conclude committee work *today*, so that members could catch flights home for the weekend." He gave her a false smile. "So your bill is scheduled to be heard right after the dinner break—tonight."

Lauren felt the smile on her face freeze. "Assemblyman Dennison requested that the chair hold over his bill until tomorrow, and Jamie promised me he would."

"Ah yes, well, while Jamie is the chair's chief of staff, she's not the chair. Over drinks last night, he was specifically asked to wrap up the committee's work today. I'm sure she'll get around to telling you."

"Who asked him?"

"My boss." Don grinned.

If she could ball up her fists and beat his puffy pink face to a pulp, she would. Her right eye started to twitch; her anger management skills were being tested. She'd been taking sessions at the insistence of her father, who pointed out that she couldn't afford another road rage incident. Instead, she took a four-count inhale along with a four-count exhale and glanced at the time on her cell phone. She had to get to Phil. He had to be notified immediately of the change in events—as well as the fact she had failed to do her job.

"Well, I've got some paperwork to take care of before the lunch break." She stood, calmed. "I'm sure I'll see you later."

He gave her a mock bow. "Without a doubt."

Minutes later, Lauren paced back and forth in front of Phil's door. She knew he could see her through the glass pane, and she knew that he was deliberately pretending he didn't hear her rapid knock. Finally, he paused from tapping on his laptop and waved her in.

"This is not a good time, Lauren," he said, not looking up and continuing to type. "I've got to get this speech written, and right now it sounds like crap. Can it wait?"

Lauren stayed standing in front of the disorder on his desk. "That's up to you; your speech may not be needed." She swallowed. "I don't think we'll have the votes for the public works bill."

He stopped tapping and stared at her.

She rushed ahead. "Phil, before you blow, I've done everything I could think of to gather the three extra votes we need." She could hear the plaintive wail in her own voice. "I'm pretty confident about Carr, but Wilson and Keller—well, I don't know."

"Then you haven't done everything."

"Phil, I—"

"You have a little less than twenty-four hours to wrap this up. You can—"

"That's another thing; we don't have twenty-four hours." She glanced down at her cell phone for the time. "We have four, maybe five hours."

"What happened?"

"I heard from Eastbrook that Mitchell convinced the chair to wrap things up tonight." She took the seat in front of his desk. "This was after Jamie promised me we'd have until tomorrow."

Phil was silent as he swiveled his chair to face out the window. It was a close-up view of the plain gray masonry wall of the adjacent building.

He spoke slowly. "Lauren, you told me that you could deliver the votes needed to pass Dennison's bill. In fact, you volunteered and browbeat me into giving you a chance because you said you would win."

"That was before the finance and public works committees merged, making a total of nineteen members, and I needed ten votes to secure a majority."

"Yeah, rough break, but that's politics. Either you can deliver, or you can't." He turned to face her. "Dennison is counting on us to cover his back. Now, it's crunch time and you're wavering. If we lose the vote count tonight, don't come back tomorrow."

They exchanged looks and Lauren gave him a small tilt of her head in acknowledgement.

He was right. Votes were what counted.

Jamie Logan's door was partially open, but Lauren could hear from the tone in her elevated voice that she was on the phone. She peeked in, and for the second time that day she waited to be waved in, but Jamie glanced up and then turned her back to the door.

Lauren opened the door wider and despite Jamie's over-the-shoulder look of sharpened daggers, took a stance in front of her desk.

"I'm sorry, I've got someone who just barged in and interrupted our conversation," Jamie informed her caller. "Let me get back to you in a few minutes."

She clicked off.

"What do you want, Lauren?"

"What I want is for you to keep our agreement," she said between clenched teeth. "I want the hearing on our bill to be held tomorrow."

"Too late, you got trumped by the democratically elected committee chair." Jamie lightened her voice. "By the way, nice shoes." She pointed down at Lauren's three-inch heels.

"My gift to myself for landing this position," Lauren responded, preening a bit. Her black patent leather pumps with their peep toes were her good luck charm. "Louboutins are the best. The dark red soles are a giveaway."

"Yeah, well, I wouldn't know. I'm a civil servant, not a consultant like you. I can't afford shoes that cost seven hundred dollars," Jamie said. She reshuffled the stack of papers in front of her and leaned over her desk. "Look, there's nothing I can do. You know how the game is played."

"First of all, they were eight hundred dollars." Lauren smiled. "And I do know the game. I know that if you do this, don't expect our vote for your agenda in the future."

"No threats, please," Jamie said, shaking her head. "The committee is adjourned for dinner. It won't reconvene until seven o'clock. I take it you need more time to get the votes?"

"Yes," Lauren admitted, sinking heavily into the chair.

"How many are you missing?"

"Three."

"*Three.* Lauren, even without the adjournment, I don't see—"

"Enough." She braced her hands against the arms of the chair and stood. "I don't have the option. If I can't secure ten ayes before the committee adjourns for the session, then I won't be here next week."

"I'm sorry, but I don't see how I—"

Lauren didn't stay to hear her finish. She had to get those votes.

***

Lisa York was sitting at her desk when Lauren poked in her head, forcing a big smile.

"Lisa, got a minute?"

"If you can talk while I eat this cold Egg McMuffin I've been trying to finish since this morning." She waved Lauren in while taking a bite of the crumpled-looking bun. "This is the first break I've had all day. I hate the end of a session. What's on your mind?"

Lauren leaned confidentially over the woman's desk. "I just wanted to close the loop to make sure your boss didn't have any questions about the public works bill."

"No, not as long as we can count on Assemblyman Dennison's vote for our water bill. Assemblywoman Carr will go along with him as long as he helps her carry her bucket of ... excuse the pun ... water."

"Good. It's going to be close," Lauren said with slight irritation.

"Ah, you've got your bill on for tonight's late session." Lisa chewed and spoke. "Don't worry about us. Despite my advisement, Assemblywoman Carr thinks the public works bill may not be *the* answer, but it's *an* answer she can support. I, on the other hand, don't trust you guys, but she's the one the people elected. Just don't forget how we came through for you."

Lauren gave her a generous smile. "I won't forget, and thank you."

Two to go.

***

Assemblyman Connor Wilson was new to the Assembly. He hadn't been elected, but was appointed by the governor to fill a seat after his predecessor resigned for medical reasons. Ordinarily, new members would spend their first couple of years on obscure committees learning the ways of the Capitol. Instead, Wilson inherited the seat of a man who had been an active leader on the Public Works Committee, one of the most powerful committees in the state.

Unfortunately, during his short tenure Wilson had succeeded in alienating not only every member of his own committee, but also two major unions and a large number of his own constituents. Most of the Capitol staff, including the ones working in the cafeteria, dreaded working with the prima donna. Wilson was president of his own fan club and a legend in his own mind.

It was no secret among staffers that Dennison had negotiated with the chair for the Public Works Committee to meet in joint session with the Public Utilities Committee. Dennison had to diffuse Wilson's vote by stacking the committee with a majority of supporters.

That morning Lauren had snuck a look at Wilson's public calendar to make sure he was at his desk and able to see her. For some reason, Wilson seemed to like her. She hated to play the role of a worshiping fan, but she had to get his vote. And since he wasn't able to keep staff longer than a single pay period, she knew he must be feeling isolated. She checked her appearance in the mirror, practiced an engaging smile, and headed to the other side of the building.

"Lauren, good to see you," said Wilson, standing next to the counter in his office suite. He reached out his hand to shake hers.

Like most legislative offices, Wilson's consisted of a private office and an outer reception area. The more seasoned members had one or two additional offices for their senior staff. Wilson's predecessor had a large office with oak-paneled walls and floor-to-ceiling bookshelves on either side of a fireplace. Unfortunately for Wilson, the Assembly leadership was able to dictate that, regardless of his new role, he would be assigned to an office that was just a little larger than the basement supply room it was located next to.

"Assemblyman." Lauren shook his hand. "Thank you for seeing me."

"Come on in, I was just getting a bite to eat." He pointed her to his small work space, consisting of a battered oak desk and two matching chairs, circa 1950. A tall metal bookshelf was the only other furniture. He didn't even have a window.

Payback is a bitch.

He picked up a sandwich. "Can I offer you a bottle of water?"

"No, nothing for me, thanks. I won't take up much of your time." She put her notebook on top of his desk and, sitting on one of the creaking chairs, rolled it forward. "I'll come right to the point. I came on behalf of Assemblyman Dennison. He hopes he has your support for his public works bill."

Wilson grinned. "Yeah, I figured that's why you're here." He wiped his mouth. "And I'm sorry I won't be able to give him my vote."

"Can I tell him why not?"

He shrugged. "It's simple. I've got to show people that I'm an independent thinker, willing to buck the tide."

Lauren took a deep breath. "Have you read the bill?"

"Er, no, my senior staff person left last week without providing me a briefing paper."

"Well, I can give you a quick summary." Lauren leaned forward. "We think AB 74 can contribute more to—"

"Lauren, Lauren, I like you, but it doesn't matter. I'm not voting for it." Wilson picked up his wrapper and napkin and tossed them in the trash. "I'll let you know something. I have a strategy; I vote aye for three bills, and then I vote no for the next three bills."

"What!"

He chuckled. "I know you must think it odd, but I've done my research. My voting record is along party lines by just sticking to this formula. It's science." He frowned. "I don't always have staff as good as you who can advise me, so I vote three 'yeses'—then three 'nos' in a cycle."

"That's unbelievable," Lauren blurted, incredulous. "What if you get it wrong and vote for a really bad bill, or, in a case like ours vote down a good bill? Are you uncomfortable with reading bill language for yourself?"

"Don't have time," he said. "Have you seen the font size on those things?" He nodded toward the clock on the wall. "Look, I've got to squeeze in a meeting with a consultant who represents a large pharmaceutical company in my district."

Lauren was amazed with his brazenness and utter stupidity.

"You know, Assemblyman, I think you're going to have to break your voting … er, strategy. You're going to give Assemblyman Dennison your vote."

"Sorry, I can't do that. I have my formula."

"Really."

She lifted up her notebook and revealed a small flat electronic recorder. She clicked a button on its front, and Wilson's voice from the last minutes came through loud and clear.

His face blanched.

Lauren watched him without sympathy. It never failed. In the political arena she found it always helped to tape conversations; things moved fast and details could be lost. And in this case, a representative of the voters could be persuaded to do his job. She was hoping to get something incriminating, but nothing this good. At least he had the sense to realize that his career was headed for the toilet. She turned off the machine.

"Assemblyman, sorry about messing up your … voting record, but I've got to depart and you have that committee meeting coming up. So, I'll leave you. Can I tell Dennison that we have your vote?"

A crestfallen Wilson nodded without speaking.

"Good."

One to go.

***

Madeline Keller was one of the smartest women in the Legislature—on either side of the aisle. At sixty-nine, she was fit, attractive, and charming. She was also a veteran Assembly member, having served over four terms in office, one of the longest in the state. With a background as a professor of public policy at Berkeley, her voting record was thoughtful and defensible. Capitol staff knew they had a winner if they had her vote.

George Kenny was her senior aide. Lauren and George had a strained relationship. She knew George didn't think much of her, even though he was always courteous and respectful. If she were to have a chance of securing Keller's vote, she would have to make sure she got her alone, out from under George's influence.

Lauren looked at her phone screen. It was almost six o'clock. All the other office staff had left for home. It was a little tricky getting George out of the office. It took disguising her voice and sending him on a wild-goose chase to the airport to meet a key donor that finally did the trick. Eventually, he would figure out it was her, but by then ….

She gave a light knock on Keller's door and a voice called out, "Come on in."

Lauren stepped into the well-appointed room. The United States flag was in one corner and the California flag in the other. Massive bookshelves formed an L-shape, ending at a large window looking out onto the Capitol lawn. In front of the window overlooking the Capitol rose garden, a large executive desk with neat stacks of paper stood next to a tall, spindly pedestal holding a brass eagle. A circular area rug depicting the four seasons in flowers anchored the room. It was a wonderful room, and Lauren looked around with admiration, taking a seat in one of the two matching walnut chairs.

"Assemblywoman, I was hoping to have just a few minutes of your time."

"Sure, Lauren, I know Byron Dennison has a bill coming up for vote today. Is that what your visit is about?"

Lauren leaned forward in her chair. "Yes, this bill has the potential to—"

"I'm sorry to interrupt you, but I don't want you to think you're going to have my vote." Keller looked genuinely disappointed. "This bill cuts an economic wound across my district. It will do less harm during good times, but if the expected downturn comes about, my constituents will be left without jobs and a future."

"But—"

"I've done my homework, Lauren, because I wanted to be able to vote yes. But I can't." Madeline took off the pair of glasses perched on her nose. "Have Byron pull the bill and bring back some amending language in the next session. I've just left him a message that I'll work with him next session to make it a stronger bill."

Lauren's lips formed a thin line and she straightened in her seat. Her right eye had begun to twitch. She hastily inhaled and exhaled, but it didn't work. She began a count to ten.

One ...

"Thank you, but next session is too late."

The assemblywoman shrugged, her arms open. "Then, I'm sorry. I can't give you my vote." She pointed to a stack of folders on the floor beside the desk. "I need to get to this before the meeting. Goodbye, Lauren."

... three ... four...

Lauren rose, nodding with understanding, but her eye was twitching crazily and her hands shook.

... seven ... eight ...

Keller looked at her with concern, and then bent down to pick up a folder from the pile on the floor.

Lauren turned quickly to leave, but as she did her trembling arm knocked against the base of the pedestal.

It teetered for an instant, then the eagle slid off and came crashing down against Madeline Keller's temple. With a look of complete surprise, the older woman fell forward, the gash in her forehead splattering blood over the papers on the floor and the edge of her desk. She slipped off her chair and fell to the floor.

... ten.

Lauren could only stare. Keller wasn't moving and a pool of blood was spreading under her head. She stepped back as it seeped forward toward her shoes.

She took a long breath to slow the rapid staccato of her heart. Checking the clock on the wall, she listened for movement in the outer office. It was quiet. She hurried to close the door.

What had she done?

She must get to the committee room, but she couldn't just leave Keller. An idea flickered through her mind: she would return after the vote and pretend to find her—a concerned staffer looking after a member.

Just then a voice came over the public announcement system that the committee was reconvening in a few minutes and members were asked to make their way to the hearing room.

Lauren looked down at the front of her clothes. She had been standing far enough away to avoid any flecks of blood. If she was careful, she could get away with this and keep her job.

She looked carefully at the desk and stepped gingerly around Keller's body, making sure there was no indication in the room of her ever being there. Minutes later, she closed the office door behind her and hurried down the empty hallway. She glanced at her phone. The session would be convening in five minutes.

There was already a crowd of public viewers, lobbyists, and staffers gathering outside the hearing room. Lauren walked up to Jamie with thumbs up. The woman gave her a puzzled look and a tentative smile. After the vote, Lauren would make a point to tell her she was going to check on Keller since it wasn't like her to miss a committee meeting.

And then—

Public testimony on the first item soon ended and now the members were asking final questions of staff. Lauren caught the eye of Don Eastbrook across the room, and gave him a smug smile. He turned away.

Poor loser.

It didn't matter, she had her votes now. She had the majority for the members present.

The chairman tapped the mic to get the noise level in the room to die down.

"If everyone would take their seats we'd like to keep this show on the road so we're not here all night." Putting his hand over the mic, he spoke to Jamie, who was sitting directly behind him. He turned back to announce, "I'd like you to amend your agendas; we have only four items remaining. The gracious representative from the 83rd District, Byron Dennison, has agreed to pull his bill until next session, when it will be reintroduced as a joint bill with Assemblywoman Keller." He looked down the table at Keller's vacant seat. "Our colleague must be running a bit late." He turned back to the front of the room. "Assemblyman Dennison, I along with the rest of the members want to thank you for the reprieve. It's a good bill that with a little work will be one we can all get behind." He gave a quick nod. "Now, next item."

Lauren's smile froze on her face. Her ears became muffled and her eyes blurred. Phil slipped into the chair beside her.

"I realized after you left that Dennison could earn more points with his fellow members, and get an easy win, by offering to wait." Phil stared straight ahead as he spoke. "At the last minute, Keller left a message that she would co-author. Mitchell said that even he would sign on. You were doing your rounds and I couldn't reach you. We'll be able to count to ten; it's a win-win. Sorry I was so hard on you earlier."

Lauren tried unsuccessfully to clear her throat.

"What's the matter, you look terrible," he said. "Hey, look, there's something going on at the door."

There was a shuffle and noise in the back of the room. Two security guards stood at the doors while a third, followed by

Jamie, entered the room, their eyes searching the floor. Lauren's eyes followed their gaze, looking down the aisle and then at her feet. The trail of red footsteps was faint on the carpet but still evident as it approached her chair.

It was amazing how close the color was to the soles of her Louboutin shoes.

One ... two...

R. Franklin James followed a career of political advocacy with writing mysteries. In 2013, her first book in Hollis Morgan Mystery series, *The Fallen Angels Book Club*, was published by Camel Press. *Sticks & Stones* and *The Return of the Fallen Angels Book Club* followed. Book four, *The Trade List*, was released in June 2016 and book five, *The Bell Tolls* will be released in May 2017.

MURDER BY CONCLUSION

SHERRY JOYCE

Delivering the daily mail inside the Capitol was seen by some of my friends as a menial task, but for me, it was a job—a dull job for which I was grateful, since it paid the bills.

Before landing this job, at age seventy, I worked at Lowe's. In retrospect, I was not cut out to know what size bolt should be used to screw in someone's toilet. I didn't live in their house, so how would I know? Seems I wasn't very good at helping people in the carpet department, where I was supposed to know how to calculate installations in square feet. Mine are size twelve and that's how I measured a room. Then they moved me to the paint department. I lasted there a week before they found out I was colorblind. Women asked me what shade of blue they should use to paint their kid's bedroom. Those blue paint samples were shades of green to me. I recommended orange, which didn't go over very well. So, after shuffling me from department to department, they moved me out the front door with two weeks' notice and a pat on the back for good luck.

More than the income, I was thrilled to spend my days in the California State Capitol, a building rich with history and neoclassical architectural beauty. Who would not gasp at the rotunda with its towering salmon pink walls? Or the murals with motifs of mythical animals? Or the massive Carrara marble statue of Queen Isabella and Columbus commemorating her decision to finance a voyage to the New World? For me, walking the mosaic floors inlaid with our state flower, the poppy, made me appreciate the artisan work that went into removing and painstakingly reinstalling each mosaic tile during the 1970s remodeling project. Being surrounded by history and those who worked here gave me a sense of immense pride.

Besides, I didn't need to know the color of walls and carpets—tour guides told me these things and I memorized them.

Piles of mail arrived each day to be sorted into mail bins, and my job was to put it in a cart with folders labeled by department. Each day kept me on my feet, rolling the cart though the hallways past the giant grizzly bear sculpture outside of the governor's office, occasionally sneaking a peek into the red-carpeted senate chamber when it was not in session, of course, and admiring the Corinthian columns and immense ceilings adorned with crystal chandeliers. I'd scramble down hallways with groin-vaulted ceilings and stone flooring so bumpy they made the mail cart's wheels behave like an errant grocery cart.

I greeted people as I passed them and stopped at each office to drop off letters, medium-size envelopes, and small packages. Some managers and administrative assistants were too busy typing at their laptops or keyboards to acknowledge my presence, but most gave me a nod or welcoming smile. If I were lucky, I'd even get a "Hello, George. How are you doing?" Not that anyone really wanted to know, but they asked as a courtesy to hear me say, "I'm doing just fine." Five years now, and my thick rubber-soled shoes have worn thin on the outer edges from walking these marbled floors. Never did I think I'd overhear more than common office chatter. Then yesterday I got the shock of my life.

As I put the mail on one of the office desks, I heard a scuffle from behind a door that was just slightly open. Angry voices arguing and the sound of crashing glass made me stop. Perhaps I should barge in and see what was going on, I thought. Nerves frazzled, I nixed that idea. I stood there frozen to the floor and couldn't help overhearing part of the conversation.

"He'll be dead by the end of the day," a man said in a gruff voice.

"How can you be so sure?" a woman stammered, banging something on a desk.

"There's no other way. We've discussed this and you agreed."

54

"Where is he now?" she asked, her angry voice demanding an answer.

"In the car in the garage," he whispered.

"I'm frightened. I don't think I can go through with it."

"You must," he insisted. "It has to be done. You can't back out now."

Then someone slammed the door shut. I stumbled over my cart, moving on as quickly as I could. My throat closed with fear. Did the two people who were planning the murder know I'd overheard their conversation? My hands shook and my mouth felt dry as chalk. Two people were murdering someone—he would be dead by the end of the day. How terrible!

My knees wobbled, and I knew I had to get to the garage. I thought of contacting security, but couldn't find anyone in the immediate hallway and didn't want to cause a panic. I considered that I also sounded like a crazy person. My mind was in a frenzy when I bumped into Mrs. Willits, who was carrying a small backpack.

"George! I'm glad I ran into you," she said. She bent over with her hand on her chest, nearly out of breath. "One of the kids on tour today left his backpack next to the grizzly bear, intent on getting a photo with a schoolmate. Could you take it to Lost and Found? I'm running late for a meeting."

"Sure. Here, let me take it."

Mrs. Willits pivoted and scurried down the hall.

I didn't want to lose any more time dealing with a lost backpack, so I threw it on top of the cart and scuttled it into the hallway utility closet, shut the door, and headed for the garage on 10th and L Street. Six levels of parked cars. Where to start looking? Most likely the man would be in the trunk, right? Aren't murderers always putting dead bodies in trunks? What if he was in a trunk with duct tape across his mouth and could not scream? What if he were drugged?

I walked the top floor of the garage first and went past each car, putting my ear to trunks, listening for any suspicious sounds. Nothing. I peered into car windows. Nothing. When other cars passed me it forced me to stand up straight and merely walk on, as if I were going to my own car instead of behaving like a potential thief. Sweat trickled down my neck. What if those two people had shot the man and he was bleeding to death? I ran to the elevator, took it to the next level, and continued looking into the cars. Perhaps I should call the police. But what would I tell them? How believable would it sound to the cops for me to say I'd overhead a conversation from two people in an office about someone who would be dead by the end of the day and was already in the garage?

Since I hadn't seen the two people talking, I couldn't identify them. Worst of all, I was not even sure *garage* meant the Capitol garage. What if it meant a house garage?

I scrambled to a slow jog, going from one car to the other. My breathing accelerated to a hefty pant. Exhausted, I had covered the fifth floor and found nothing worrisome. I ran down the stairwell to the fourth floor, certain by now the man would be gasping his last breath. How long could air last in a trunk? What if he were gagged and couldn't even whimper? What if his feet were bound and he couldn't kick the top of the trunk to make a sound? Did he know about punching out a taillight? I'd seen that in a movie. But then I ruled that out because one had to have a free foot to accomplish such a feat. Gasping, I started zigzagging from car to car to make sure I was checking parked cars on each side of the floor. Nothing suspicious. No blood dripping from a trunk either.

I tore down the stairs to the third floor, sure time was running out. I considered what I'd overheard and decided this had to be a love triangle. That's the way it worked on television.

Maybe this scoundrel deserved to die. Perhaps he had lured the wife into a sordid affair and she had confessed everything to her husband. Maybe I had it backwards. Oh gosh … that could be it. Maybe the two people talking in the office were the ones having the affair and it was her husband they were trying to kill. That had to be it. Her husband found out and had to be done away with. I smacked myself on my forehead with my hand, as if a bright light of intelligence had just struck me. But I wasn't watching where I was going. A car backed out, didn't see me, and hit me in the side of the hip. In an instant I was flat out on the ground.

"Are you OK?" the driver yelled, bending down to cradle my head. Blood was dripping from the side of my face where I had slammed into the pavement.

"Yes, I'm OK, but I think I've broken my hip."

"I'm calling nine-one-one," she said. "I'm a nurse and your breathing is very rapid. I think you are having a heart attack."

"No, no," I stammered. "I was running from floor to floor looking for a body."

She gave me an odd, disconcerting look befitting a crazy person before the garage lights went dim and then dark, peacefully dark.

I didn't feel the paddles that jolted me back to earth, but now the oxygen mask was on my face. I grabbed at it, trying to pull it off, but the attendant in the ambulance insisted on keeping it on my face. I mumbled into breathy fog, "There is a man in a car in the garage about to die," and then I watched the ambulance ceiling spin circles. A needle was stuck in my arm, blood or saline dripping. Here I was going to the hospital and someone else would be dead—a murder I couldn't stop.

***

When I awoke in the hospital, I had a fractured pelvis, a split lip, and a terrible headache from a mild concussion. Mummy-like tape covered my hips and I was in some sort of traction device. I frantically pushed the call button too many times until a disgruntled nurse arrived.

"Yes, what do you need?" She scowled at me, checking my vitals on various machines.

"I want to report a murder," I blurted out, realizing it sounded deranged.

"You killed someone?"

"No, no. I didn't kill anyone, but I overheard two people planning on killing her husband."

"I think you're hallucinating. You've been on a lot of drugs," she suggested, pressing some lever to raise my head up.

"No, really. I overheard two people at work discussing the demise of someone in the parking lot—someone in the car who wouldn't last much longer. I think the body was in a trunk."

The nurse, Brandy, looked at me with utmost concern. I found her name humorous, since my behavior might seem as if I had been the one drinking.

"If you're really concerned about a murder, I suggest you call the police. I'll dial the phone for you if you want me to."

I rolled my eyes in a grateful nod, while she dialed 911 and handed me the phone.

"Hello. What is your emergency?"

"My name is George Dillard and I work at the Capitol in the mail room."

"That doesn't sound serious."

"Well, it is. I was pushing the mail cart around the halls and I overheard a conversation between a man and a woman in one of the staff offices, talking about murdering someone whose body was in the garage and would not last much longer."

"Seriously?"

"Don't you take callers seriously?" I asked her in a scornful tone.

"Of course, Mr. Dillard. I'm sorry. I'm a summer intern. This is my first day on the job. Where are you calling from?"

"I'm in Sutter Hospital."

"Psychiatric ward?"

"No, for goodness' sake. I don't like your humor. I've broken my pelvis."

"Were you part of the murder scene?"

"Gosh, no! You've got this all wrong. Please send someone to the Capitol now and check the garage floors. The body is in the trunk of a car—he probably won't last much longer."

"How long ago did you hear about this murder plot?"

I glanced at my watch. It was now four. I recalled hearing the conversation just after my shift began.

"Around eight thirty," I mumbled. "But he's probably dead by now."

"But you didn't kill him?"

"No, of course not. How many times do I have to tell you the story?"

"OK. I'll send someone to the Capitol. What floor and what office did you hear the conversation coming from?"

Main floor, budget office, first door on your left. Hurry, please. He doesn't have much time to live."

"Who doesn't?"

"The guy in the car."

"Yes, you've mentioned that. You don't know him, right?"

"Of course not, you dolt."

"Sir, please don't be rude. I'm here to help. We get a lot of crank calls, and this one is borderline, as I'm sure you can understand. Why are you in the hospital again?"

"I got hit by a car in the parking garage."

"You were in the garage during the murder, sir?"

"No, you're an idiot. I was trying to save the guy's life."

"You knew the man?"

"No, I've never met him. How could I? He's the woman's husband."

"So, the woman's husband is in the car?"

"Yes, yes, and he's probably dead by now."

"Where's the wife?"

"How should I know? She's probably with her lover, who is committing the murder."

"Oh, right. I should have picked up on that."

"You're not taking me seriously, miss."

"Mr. Dillard, I'm trying. Please give me your number and I'll pass it on the officer who will investigate. He'll probably want to talk with you."

"I would hope so. Please tell the officer I want to know if the man is dead or not. These two can't get away with this."

"They're going somewhere?"

"Well, wouldn't you if you killed someone?"

"I suppose. I've never thought about it."

"They need to flip me over now, so I have to go."

"Flip you over?"

"Never mind. You wouldn't understand."

The sound of the phone clicking dead was refreshing. I could feel pain meds kicking in, dripping into my veins like a welcome cocktail of relief from all of this distress. Sleep started to overcome me, fogging up my brain to where I could no longer focus. I shook my head to stay awake.

***

"I need to take your temperature, Mr. Dillard."

"Uh huh. Can you please turn on the TV for me?" I glanced at my watch and realized I had slept for three hours. Besides aching, I was ravenous for a steak, which I knew would not be forthcoming. I pulled the pillow up under my head to get a better view of the TV and clicked the controller until I found the KCRA 3 nightly news. In my stupor I saw a reporter. She was at the Capitol.

"This is Edie Lambert reporting from the Capitol on a strange series of events. The Capitol had to be evacuated today because of a bomb scare. An unattended backpack was found by a department secretary when she entered a utility closet looking for office supplies. The bomb squad was called and the backpack was dismantled on the front lawn. It contained nothing but schoolbooks and a metal thermos. Tension was high, but everyone was relieved to return to work. Then, later today, George Willard, an employee from the mail room, called the police from the hospital regarding a potential murder plot he'd overheard at work earlier in the morning in which the victim was supposedly in the Capitol parking garage. George took it upon himself to investigate the cars in the garage when he was accidentally hit by a driver backing out of a parking stall. George landed in the hospital with a broken hip, but is reported doing well.

"Officers on the scene checked all the cars in the garage and reported finding an old dog on a large, soft bed, comfortably asleep in a large SUV, windows opened for air on a chilly day.

From his dog tags, we found the owners of the dog, who worked at the Capitol. The husband and wife were very upset about having to put Murphy down because of his advanced cancer. John and Jessica Bradford both work at the Capitol and were arguing about it this morning, struggling with the decision. Mr. Bradford told me their veterinarian had suggested they put him to sleep this morning, but Jessica wanted one more day with Murphy. They took him to work in the SUV so he'd be close by during lunch and they could spend some final hours with him. Murphy passed away quietly this evening in the arms of two people who loved him dearly. Reporting from the Capitol, this is Edie Lambert, KCRA 3. Gulstan, back to you."

I shut off the TV, stunned at the turn of events. No bomb. No murder. No affair. How could I have been so wrong? Like Jack Bauer, I had wanted to solve this myself—I should have told someone. Things are not always what they seem. No doubt I'd seen too many cop shows on TV and read too many crime novels to spice up my somewhat dull life as a mail delivery person.

***

Later that day, John and Jessica Bradford drove home in silence. He chewed on the inside of his cheek and kept his eyes deliberately focused ahead on the road.

"I'm sorry about the affair." Jessica sniffled and wiped tears from her eyes.

"I shouldn't have hit him with the lamp—but when I saw the two of you together, my blood boiled."

Jessica sighed and turned toward John. "Do you plan to bury them together?"

"Why not? As soon as I get him out of the trunk of your car, I'll bury him with Murphy. Grave's already dug in the woods."

Sherry Joyce's contemporary romantic suspense novels delicately balance themes of love, danger, loss and survival. Her characters are flawed, human and seek justice, making readers turn pages set in some of the most romantic settings in the world. *The Dordogne Deception*, her debut novel is set in England and a castle in southwestern France. *Dangerous Duplicity* explores family strength in a yachting dynasty. She lives in Eldorado Hills with her husband and beloved Westies.

DANGER IN CAPITAL LETTERS

TERESA LEIGH JUDD

The note arrived in her mail.

In bold print, the warning was ominous: "GIVE IT BACK OR ELSE!"

Lisa looked at the envelope. No return address. Her name and address in block letters on the front. She shook her head. Give back what? To whom? Or else what? It must have been sent to the wrong person, she thought. She tossed it in the wastebasket and forgot about it.

The next night as she approached her front door, she heard her phone ringing. She rushed in and grabbed the receiver.

"Hello."

To her dismay, a computerized voice said, "You've been warned. Leave it behind the potted plant on your front porch."

"Wait," she said. "Leave what?"

But the caller had disconnected. She went to the wastebasket and retrieved the note, hoping there was some clue as to what the unknown person or persons wanted, but it was still as inscrutable as when she first looked at it. She wracked her brain trying to think of something she might have taken by mistake, but nothing occurred to her.

This is getting a little scary, she thought. Whoever they are, they know where I live.

She had only put the potted chrysanthemums on the front porch of her townhouse in Midtown Sacramento less than a week before. She wondered if she should call the police. But what could they do with so little information? She would look like a fool if it was just someone playing a joke on her.

The next night when the phone rang, she nervously picked up the receiver. "Hello?"

63

"Hey, Lisa, it's Katie. I was wondering if you wanted to go out for drinks tonight. I'm getting bored hanging around home."

"Katie," Lisa breathed a sigh of relief. "I would love to go out. I sort of need to get away myself." She figured she'd tell Katie about the note and phone call once they were settled in a cozy bar someplace. "Where do you want to meet?"

"That new wine bar in Old Town looks nice. About seven?"

"Perfect. I'll see you there."

Once they were comfortably ensconced in a booth, wine glasses in hand, Lisa described the incidents to her friend. Neither of them could come up with anything at all in the way of an explanation.

"It was probably just a prank," Katie said.

But Lisa wasn't so sure. When she returned home later that evening, she was proved right. As she attempted to put her key in the lock, she noticed the lock seemed damaged. She pushed the door open and gasped as she turned on the light. The room had been taken apart. Pillows were slashed. Books with the spines broken were scattered on the floor. DVDs littered the living room. Drawers had been pulled out of cabinets and even the kitchen had been searched. The large containers of flour and sugar that decorated her counters had been emptied on the floor. Afraid that someone might still be upstairs in the house, she backed out and called 911.

The police came and established that whoever had been there was now gone. Pulling out his notebook, one of the officers asked her name and where she worked.

"I am an administrative assistant in Assemblyman Newland's office."

"Can you tell if anything is missing?"

"Nothing obvious. I might discover something after I've cleaned up the mess. I'll certainly report it if I do. I think I should tell you that this is the third strange incident I've had lately. I received a note asking me to return something, and the next day there was a threatening phone call, then this. I think it's a case of mistaken identity. I haven't got anything that could possibly trigger this reaction."

"Can I see the note?"

"I'm sorry, I threw it away."

"All right, I'll file the report, and you let us know if anything more happens. In the meantime, I recommend you have better locks installed."

When she was alone, she looked at the mess, slumped into a chair, and covered her eyes. Why was this happening to her? What did they want? After a restless night, Lisa dragged herself, red-eyed and exhausted, into work the next morning.

Jake, her immediate boss, noticed she looked a little bedraggled and asked if she was OK.

"My townhouse was broken into last night," she said. "I've been getting threats, telling me to give back something, but I don't know what I'm supposed to give back. So they searched my house, I guess. I don't know if they found what they were looking for. I don't know what to do."

"Oh, my gosh. I'm so sorry to hear this. You don't know what they want?"

"No. If I did, I would definitely give it back," Lisa said.

"Yeah, I guess you would. Whatever it is, it's not worth keeping if you're being threatened. You've tried to think what it might be?"

"It's all I think about."

"Well, let me know if there's anything I can do," Jake said, turning back toward his office.

"Maybe now that they've searched the house, they'll leave me alone," Lisa murmured to herself.

Unfortunately, this did not turn out to be the case.

It was dark by the time Lisa pulled up in front of her house. As she exited the car, a large man grabbed her arm and threw her on the ground.

"We've asked you nicely," he growled. "Give me the thumb drive or I'm going to have to hurt you."

"Thumb drive?" Lisa cried. "What thumb drive?"

"You know what thumb drive," he said.

"No, no. Please. I don't know what you're talking about."

"Right," he said, kicking her in the ribs. She put her arm up to protect her face, and he smashed her arm with his foot.

"I don't know what you want," Lisa whimpered, and then she passed out.

When she woke up, she was in a hospital. She hurt all over.

A nurse bent over her. "I see you're awake."

"What happened?" Lisa asked.

"You were found in front of your townhouse. Looks like you were mugged. A neighbor called an ambulance. You have several broken ribs and a broken arm. Do you know who did this?"

"No," Lisa said. "I wish I did."

"Now that you're awake, there's a policeman waiting to take your statement. I'll go get him," the nurse said. She left the room and returned with a uniformed officer, who dutifully took down what little Lisa could tell him.

The next morning, she called into work. Her boss, Jake, answered the phone.

"I won't be in today," she said. "I'm in the hospital."

"Oh no, Lisa. What happened?"

"A big guy attacked me in front of my house. Wanted me to give him a thumb drive. I can't begin to think of a thumb drive I have that anyone would want." She gave a little sob. "I don't think this nightmare is ever going to end."

"Maybe after searching your house and beating you up, they'll be convinced that you don't have whatever they are looking for."

"I can only hope you're right," she said. "I don't want to have to leave town. Anyway, I'll be back in as soon as they release me."

And, miraculously, as Jake had predicted, there were no more threats. No more attacks.

At first, Lisa jumped at every unexpected sound. She approached her house and car with stealth and caution, but after a few weeks she finally began to feel safe. Whoever had been threatening her seemed to have gone away.

Her sister was expecting a baby, and the shower was to be held the following weekend. Lisa dug the bag of baby gifts out of the closet and began to sort them for wrapping. As she lifted out a baby blanket, a thumb drive fell onto the bed.

She had shopped for the gifts during one of her lunch hours, and couldn't resist showing them to her fellow office workers. She had spread them all out on her desk, and the women oohed over each item as she pulled it out. As they examined her purchases, Jake hurried into the room, followed by Assemblyman Newland. The other women strolled away, but Jake suddenly took an interest in the baby clothes, picking up a onesie and some booties. She thought this a little out of character. Still, he helped her put them all back in the bag while Newland gave them a "get back to work" glare.

Now, she picked up the thumb drive and saw it had no identifying label. Curious, she slipped it into her computer and was appalled to find out it was a recording of a conversation that had taken place in the assemblyman's office. He was talking to the head of a local construction company. They were apparently planning on fixing a bid so the company would get a particularly lucrative state job in exchange for a hefty contribution to the legislator's reelection fund. Jake could be heard in the background occasionally.

She realized Jake was the only person with an opportunity to slip the thumb drive into the bag. Probably planning on a little blackmail, he'd needed to hide it when the boss followed him into the room. He would have thought he could retrieve it later that day, but as it happened she had taken the bag down to the parking garage and locked it in her car.

***

The next morning she entered Jake's office and shut the door behind her.

"Did I mention that when I was being beat up, the guy asked for a thumb drive? This thumb drive, maybe?" she asked, dangling the USB stick in front of him. "I can't believe you would have me beaten up and my apartment ransacked. You could just have asked me if I had found it in the bag because you were pretty sure it had slipped in there. I'd have been no wiser."

"Did you listen to it?" he asked.

"Yes. Pretty incriminating language, I'd say. What were you thinking?"

"I'm so sorry." Jake looked down at his desk. "I told Newland and the owner of the construction company that I had taped evidence they were in collusion. In exchange for certain perks, I'd see that it never saw the light of day. They agreed to my request, but demanded I give them the tape immediately, which I did. But then I told them I had made a backup copy to ensure nothing happened to me. They got really angry. Either give them the copy or else something would definitely happen to me. I let it slip that I thought it had gone home with you by accident. I never thought the construction company owner would send someone after you. And once they started threatening you, I didn't dare say anything. I mean, you could have me charged with all kinds of felonies."

"So you just let them threaten me and attack me?" Lisa asked. "I can't believe you're so low."

"Well, I did get them to stop when I heard what they were doing. I told them you had already confided in me that you didn't know what thumb drive they wanted or where it might be, but when it did turn up, I was sure you would let me know. Then I could take steps to get it back. Say it was mine, and it was all a misunderstanding."

"So, they went for that?"

"Yes. They agreed to lay off you until it turned up. Now I can tell them you found it and hand it over to them. I'll say that although you were curious as to its content, you were afraid to listen to it. You didn't want to be involved in any way."

"Will they believe you? What if they think I did listen to it?"

"Even if you did, without the thumb drive as proof, it would be just your word against theirs, and they could paint you as a disgruntled government employee attempting to extort money from them. There might be some awkward questions, but no hard evidence. Then Newland could just fire you. As long as you don't say anything, they'll assume they are safe. So, now that you know, what are you going to do?"

"It's not what I'm going to do. It's what you're going to do."

"What do you mean?"

Lisa carefully slid the thumb drive into her pocket.

"You are going to resign your position here and give a public statement to the papers that you had discovered the collusion between Newland and the construction company and could no longer work under such conditions."

"Resign? But—but—I can't do that. I need this job," Jake said. "And, if the assemblyman is removed from office, you'll lose your job, too."

"Hey, you'll come out as a hero whistle-blower. I'm sure you'll get another job. And there are plenty of honest assemblymen needing office help. I'm not worried. Anyway," she patted her pocket, "it's resign OR ELSE."

Teresa Leigh Judd, an awarding-winning short story writer, has had stories in each of Capitol Crimes' anthologies, as well as publication in online and other print collections. Inspired by the "dragons" found among us, she created *Dragon Tales*, a short story collection published in 2014, and available in print and ebook. For more information, see her website: www.TeresaLeighJudd.com.

BLACK SHEEP

VIRGINIA V. KIDD

You know how every family has a black sheep? Ours is my younger sister, Melanie. Yes, the twenty-six-year-old with the golden ringlets that cascade down to frame eyes the blue of a Sacramento summer sky, eyes rimmed in thick, dark lashes that not all the mascara at Nordstrom could create for me. That one.

As inured as our family has become to the mortifying, life-disrupting decisions that sprout without warning out of what passes for her brain, we never expected her to be charged with murder.

She called me. She gets one call, and she picks me when she could have dialed a good criminal attorney or at least Dad, who knows good criminal attorneys. No, I was the one jolted out of sleep at 2:43 a.m. to hear, "Oh, Janine, I truly cannot imagine why they're charging me with killing Ryan because I was, like, holding the knife. I picked it up, you know, since it has jewels on the handle, real jewels not just glass, and I mean you don't just leave something like that lying on those wooden sidewalks of Old Sacramento, do you, but that doesn't mean I used it. Go by my apartment and get me a fresh shirt, OK? This one is all bloody. Bring the new plum one that has a big heart in rhinestones."

Oh, sure. You want to look your best when they snap your mug shot.

She didn't call Dad, but I did. Turns out she wasn't officially charged yet, just teetering on the brink. After arranging for her to legally leave the scene and calling a lawyer, Dad, wily manipulator that he is, dropped her off at my Midtown apartment and sped away, probably fleeing with Mom to that beach beyond the Coastal Ranges where his cell phone doesn't work.

My apartment was built in the late 1930s. It has hardwood floors, ivory beadboard walls, scalloped cornices, and built-in bookshelves hugging a fireplace. In that setting, Melanie looked like an actress who had wandered onto the wrong stage. Crystal earrings dangled from multiple ear holes and a sapphire glittered from one eyebrow. Her plum, rhinestone-imprinted tee, which Dad had taken her, topped a filmy ecru mini-skirt above black lace tights with a pattern of scattered inkblot tests. Her shoes had red four-inch heels, soles, and little else but ribbons. I stood there in my jeans, T-shirt, and REI sandals, trying to figure out how her shoes stayed on her feet.

"I'm not a child," she told me. This was in reference not to her situation but to the Cheerios I offered for a belated breakfast.

"Take it or leave it, Melanie."

It was typical of Melanie to ignore the bowl I had set on the table and go grab a red one from the kitchen counter, saying, "So much prettier. Why not enrich life in little ways when we can?" She gave me her "aren't I special" smile. I just watched her pour in cereal and milk and said nothing. My gray tabby, Cat Choo, sat up with a low growl. The red bowl was his.

I settled at the table across from her, coddling my warm mug of Italian roast, breathing in its scent like aroma therapy. Outside, a distant train whistle marked the Capitol Corridor Amtrak chugging early risers to the Bay Area. I pictured them as heavy-eyed as I was, clutching lattes like Linus blankets.

"What happened last night, Melanie?"

"Ryan was stabbed with that beautiful knife those police officers took. Things didn't work out for Ryan and me, we were breaking up, but I liked him. I can't see why anyone would stab him. We'd all been getting along so well, working together. Ryan loved my ideas." She paused, blinking rapidly, her face looking for just one moment heartbreakingly young.

"Start at the beginning." I heard my voice soften.

"Five of us were there." She spooned up cereal.

"Where?"

"First at the Firehouse for dinner, and, oh, Janine, you should eat there sometime. If you ever find true love or even half-true love like Ryan and I had, that's the place to go. Even if you just get a date—"

"Skip the advice on my love life. Who was there?"

"Ryan and me, Brandon, Courtney, and Nick. You met them at my Christmas party, except Nick. You should see him." She smiled one of the smiles that sets off alarms in our family. "Tall, piercing blue eyes, thick dark hair, rugged jaw—he's such a hunk! They're all Ryan's friends. I mean, except for the one who killed him."

I conjured up the guests I met last December, Ryan first. Stocky, with red-blond hair and the sunburned-looking skin that goes with it, he'd still had the quick grin and eager face of a kid about to dive in the pool. And the others? I said, "Brandon is the loud, ex-football player who can't let it go, right? The chunky one with the fake sun streaks in his hair who's always talking and needs to be right all the time."

Melanie glared at me. "Brandon is friendly. He's in real estate, and his ties to football are useful."

"And Courtney's the skeleton-thin one who always dresses like she's going to a funeral."

"Black is *in*, Janine. She's a graphic designer. Her look is arty." She slid her glare toward Cat Choo. "Your wretched cat keeps staring at me. Make him stop."

Oh, sure. "I don't understand about the knife. Who brings a knife on a dinner date?"

"He brought it to show us. It's an art piece more than a knife and very expensive. Real gold and silver swirls on each end of the handle with tiny diamonds and rubies down the center. There's something special about the blade, too, but I didn't pay attention to that. Ryan planned to sell it to help fund our business."

I steeled myself. "What business?"

"Capitol Caps. We'll sell caps that look like the dome of the Capitol building. Isn't that brilliant?"

I stared. "With a bill, like a ball cap?"

"Exactly! Ryan loved the idea when I suggested it. The cap dome is bigger than a regular ball cap, of course, and has a cupola on the very top with a gold ball like the real cupola. The bill is the green Capitol grounds. Protesters can write their slogans there, like they were marching with signs. It's a perfect souvenir of the capital city. And useful too. With all the media hype about sun damage, these will sell out in no time."

Really? Wearing the State Capitol on your head? "How is your business funded?"

"We're our own backers. Courtney provided—they called it 'seed money,' and she did our advertising campaign. Kind of plain, I thought, so I fixed it. Nick has savings. He knows computer stuff, so I guess he has money. Brandon expected to get funds soon from some deal, and Ryan was selling the knife and some antiques."

By my count that was four donors. "What about you?"

"Oh, Janine! People can get advances on credit cards, surely even you know that!"

I took a deep breath. "So you all examined the knife, ate dinner, and then what?"

"We strolled toward the river. We crossed that awful street full of rocks that are just death on shoes. Are they ever going to pave that thing?"

"No! Those are cobblestones. They're historic."

"Oh, please! Can't people get over the past? I'm lucky my shoes stayed on."

I had to agree with her on that. I still couldn't figure out how they worked.

She stretched in her chair, her long arms reaching up toward the 1930s chandelier with the deep blue and orange pansies. "I need more coffee," she yawned. "I got hardly any sleep."

I took her mug and crossed to my new Keurig to make a fresh cup.

She said, "We stopped over where people wait for the excursion train. The office is closed at night, you know, so the area was empty. It was dark there; I didn't like it. An argument broke out in the group. Nick and Courtney were a little snotty about all the money not being in. I mean, can you believe it? They already had money to invest; we had to raise it. I told them to just chill, it would work out. Everybody milled around for a while. Then I heard a sort of choking moan, and Ryan"— she swallowed—"he suddenly slumped sideways. He grabbed my shoulder and leaned into me. That's how I got bloody. Then he fell, and that knife just dropped at my feet, so I picked it up." I heard a catch in her voice.

To give her a minute, I sipped my coffee, grateful for the caffeine I imagined conveying reinforcements to my waning energy force. "Melanie, didn't you see anything when Ryan was stabbed? He was murdered right there in front of you—"

"Not in front of me. I was turned away petting the dog. And you know what, Janine, I felt that dog's furry body go all stiff suddenly, like he knew."

I took a deep breath. *The dog?* Talking with Melanie was like working a fill-in-the-blank puzzle. "What dog did you pet, Melanie?"

"The blind man's Seeing Eye dog, a black lab."

My big-sister response shot out automatically. "You're not supposed to pet working service dogs. You know that."

Her eyes rolled. "The man was blind, Janine! He couldn't see me."

Even as I brought her fresh coffee, she waved the cup away. "Don't keep shoving coffee down me. I need a mondo nap. I deserve to sleep after the night I went though."

"I deserve to know what went on before you woke me during that night."

"Well, you can find out all your little heart desires over early lunch. I invited Nick, Courtney, and Brandon to come here. And don't get that stricken-hostess look! You don't need to heat up that pizza that's been in your freezer since Elvis left the building. They're bringing Chinese."

I don't know about you, but I'm not really all that thrilled at the prospect of likely murderers dropping by for lunch, even if they do bring food.

Melanie rose. "I'm napping in your room with the door shut so Cat Choo can't stare at me. He's creeping me out."

My cell rang as the bedroom door closed. "How's your sister?" Dad barked.

"Taking a nap. She said she had a bad night and needs her rest."

I heard a loud snort from the other end. "She call the lawyer?"

"Not that I know of."

"See what you can find out, Janine. A detective named Locato is in charge."

"Why me? Where are you, Dad?"

Crackling noises followed with the words, "… breaking up," "can't hear …," and "her attorney" interspersed, then the call went dead.

Did I have time to check out the scene of the crime? I glanced at my watch; it was still early. Days apparently work that way when you get up before dawn. I glanced up to find Cat Choo on the table finishing off the last of Melanie's cereal. He wasn't supposed to get up there, but in a world where a suspected murderer could steal his food bowl with impunity, it seemed a small offense. I slipped on a jacket against the cool morning and headed down to Old Sacramento.

Gray mist covered the sky and a light fog floated damp air up from the river. Night revelers were long gone and tourists yet to arrive, so parking was easy. I stepped out into a quiet city, the silence marred only by rolling traffic on Tower Bridge. Noting a bevy of police cars huddled halfway down Front Street I headed that way. It was easy to tell who was in charge. Locato looked to be about fifty, with thinning light brown hair, a pudgy, lined face, squinty eyes and an expanding middle covered by the kind of suit coat you buy at Sears. I could guess who the man beside him was, too: he stood with a black lab in a harness.

I told Locato about my poor, sweet, forlorn sister at home weeping in despair.

He barely restrained the same snort Dad made on the phone. The young officer beside him, however, said, "Gee, she was so pretty." Tall, thin, and lightly freckled, he made me think of a kid in an ad for peanut butter, now grown up.

"Calvin—" Locato shook his head.

"I'm sure she didn't stab anyone," I said, and with surprise realized I meant it. "Didn't anybody there see anything?"

"Clammed up, all of them," Locato snarled. "Only good citizen in the bunch is Mr. Grudin here."

Grudin, with his white cane and attentive black lab, could hardly be called a promising witness. About fifty and starting to bald, he wore casual slacks, a long-sleeve gray tee, and wraparound sunglasses. When his hand stretched out directly toward me, I let out a surprised, "Oh" and shook hands. He grinned. "Legally blind, not totally without sight. I can see forms."

Locato walked away with Grudin, leaving Calvin to deal with me. "What was Grudin doing there?" I asked him. "Front Street with its cobblestones isn't easy to navigate."

"I think he was there to meet with the group. Lieutenant'll find out."

Police tape cordoned off the murder scene. Calvin walked the outer circumference with me, revealing nothing I didn't already know, and I learned nothing from the scene. Finally, I told him about "the suspects" gathering at my place for lunch and gave him the address. With luck, he'd appear and stop anyone from getting ideas about my cutlery.

By the time I got home, Melanie was freshly showered and dressed, with her plum shirt tucked into a pair of my jeans. They were too short for her tall legs and stayed up around her slim waist with the help of my bright Guatemalan belt pulled tight, a visual proclamation that her waist was just oh, so much thinner than mine.

"You need new eyeliner," she said. "Yours got broken. And really, Janine—drugstore makeup?"

The doorbell rang.

Ryan's friends arrived as a group, wrapped in the fragrance of orange chicken, chow mein, and stir-fried prawns. They were in their late twenties, decked out in the very latest fashion.

Courtney held true to her love of black, both in clothes and heavy eyeliner accenting her dark eyes. Her raven hair jutted out in multiple directions in a style that was apparently intentional rather than her having forgotten to brush it. Now that I knew Brandon was "in real estate," he morphed into my stereotype of a salesman, a bit too friendly, a bit too loud. Nick, of the thick, dark hair and rugged jaw, moved with the casual swagger of John Travolta in *Grease,* a walk I thought of as the strut of attractive males who've gotten what they want from birth.

Settled around my table, they turned to the logical topic of conversation. I poured myself a Coke and leaned against the kitchen doorframe, overtly eavesdropping.

Courtney said, "This just can't be real. All the work we did, plans, designs, promotion layouts—so much is messed up."

Nick spoke up, his voice deep. "Timing is screwed."

"It's like a bad dream." Brandon swigged down beer from a six-pack he brought. "Ryan's death will sure slow down our business plan."

Slow down your business plan? These were the kind of people who would rule Wall Street some day, I thought.

Melanie chimed in, "Our plan for CAP-tivating Caps."

Courtney's dark brows slid together. "We don't call it that."

"I do," Melanie answered. "I think it's brilliant."

She grinned at Nick, but Courtney replied, her voice harsh and unyielding. "Our business is called Capitol Caps, Melanie. It's not something you can change." She stabbed at a prawn with her chopsticks.

I asked, "How could you all stand right there together and not see Ryan stabbed?"

"We didn't all stand together," Brandon snapped. "We were upset and walked off from each other. No big deal. A typical business disagreement."

"We were just calming down," Nick added.

"Dealing with funding gets frustrating," Courtney said, "especially when not everyone has the same business acumen." Her voice carried the tightness of accusation.

Suddenly, Melanie screeched, "Stop that, you claw-footed sneak thief!"

Cat Choo shot across the table and down the hall, a captured prawn clamped firmly between his teeth.

"Well, he's a cat, Melanie," Nick said with a shrug. "What do you expect? We should have given him some."

What a nice young man. I hoped he wasn't a murderer.

I heard a car door slam and peered out to see a Ford Crown Victoria at the curb. Locato stared our way as he slipped on his jacket. Calvin waited.

There's nothing like police tramping in to put a damper on a luncheon. Forks and chopsticks clattered to the table. Chairs gored scratches into my hardwood floor as seated diners scooted around to face the officers. Melanie snaked toward Nick, chair and all.

I offered the detectives seats, but the two opted to remain standing in the arch between living and dining areas. "Need to get a couple of things straight," Locato said. "Thought with you all here we could find out exactly where everybody stood at the critical time last night."

Diners exchanged glances, then carefully looked away from each other.

"Now you four and your—uh—the victim were all standing around in that waiting area. Nobody else there, you said. Right?"

He waited.

Melanie caved. "Well—" She stopped, reaching to her hair for comfort the way she did as a child, twisting a curl around a finger.

"Yeah?"

"Nothing."

"Oh, come on!" Locato barked. "Think we didn't talk to Hugh Grudin?"

Melanie's voice came out in a whisper. "I don't know who that is."

79

Locato's style was not designed to win friends. Calvin, apparently still besotted with my sister, came to her aid. "The blind man with the dog."

"Licorice." She flashed Calvin a smile. "He called the dog Licorice."

"The man with the money," Locato said. "Unless anyone else here brought $7,000 with them to buy"—he twisted his mouth to make his own next word dubious—"artwork." His eyes circled the group, one by one, his lips curled in a sneer. I had a sudden flash of him studying a drawing of Superman staring through steel, and practicing the look in a mirror.

He moved over to the end of the table. "Grudin was on the street in front of you. He could see enough and hear enough to give us the picture. The five of you got in an argument. You separated. At one point, one was on either side across from each other. Three stood together. Lots of argument and waving arms in that mix, but not so much you couldn't see a man fall."

He used his Superman stare again, sliding from face to face. I had considered the technique a joke, but it actually seemed to be working, judging from the wriggling, the short breaths, and the napkins raised to hairlines to dab at sweat.

"Turns out the wrong person got murdered," Locato almost drawled. "Hard luck for Ryan. And for the killer, too. Meant to get someone else. One of you." He paused to let that sink in. "Maybe the two off to the sides were looking away. Maybe." His voice had a gravelly tone to it now, as if his throat had tightened. "One of you saw the blade coming and ducked. You have to know who used it. You owe it to Ryan to tell us who it was, but if you don't care about that, you owe it to your own survival. The killer can find another time and place."

He waited, and I waited too, having trouble catching my breath. Hugh Grudin was legally blind. He could see shadows and forms. He could see a flash of light on a knife and a human form crouching down to avoid it. In his mind, one caused the other.

I could picture another version: a blithely unaware young woman squatting to pet a dog at just the right moment to accidentally save her life.

And never even knowing it.

"Licorice!" I choked out. "Melanie, who stood beside you when you bent to pet the dog?"

"He licked my hand," she defended, shooting a fearful glance at the officers. "I know I shouldn't have, but—"

"It's OK," I calmed her. "You're not in trouble for petting a guide dog. It's OK."

She gave me a tremulous half smile. Nick reached out and gently touched her shoulder.

"Melanie, who was beside you?" I repeated.

She sat up straight, her ringlet abandoned. Eyes filling, she slowly turned toward Locato. "Ryan," she almost whispered, and we leaned in to hear. "Ryan on one side and—Courtney on the other." Realization seemed to slide onto her face. "Courtney. It was Courtney."

"You liar!" Courtney's denial echoed off the beadboard walls. "She'll say anything for attention."

Melanie's eyes remained fixed on Courtney without blinking as if she had trained with Cat Choo.

Nick's voice trickled out, like he was grasping at bits of a slowly emerging memory. "When Melanie screamed— remember, Brandon? I was over by the train tracks and you— you were looking at the Delta King. If that's when it happened—" He stopped.

Fear coated Courtney's voice. "Then only Melanie Sunshine and I were left? Is that what you're saying, Nick?"

"Well … yes, I guess so."

Melanie remained silent, so I spoke for her. "Witnesses saw Melanie squatting down. Isn't that true? She's the one who ducked?"

Locato nodded. "Seems like it."

Courtney spoke, her voice escalating as she talked. "We weren't playing a game! It was a serious business! Did any of you realize that? You can't play around with other people's funds. No changing the name, wimping out on money, damaging the ad layout." She turned to Melanie. "You were the worst! Flirting with Ryan to get your way, dribbling my investment down the drain! You don't know shit, and Ryan listened to you."

Locato's lips tightened as if he found the scene distasteful. "Calvin—"

In two strides, Calvin was behind Courtney, jerking her up to thrust her slender wrists into handcuffs. She sagged. Her voice faded. "I just couldn't stand it anymore. The knife was in my hand, it was dark, I was so frustrated. It was just—I just wanted to be rid of her. We could do so much once I got rid of Melanie. I never wanted to hurt Ryan."

I don't think Melanie heard her. Nick held her against his chest, and her sobs covered the voice.

I thought that was the end of the story. I would certainly be content to never hear of those people or their venture ever again. But the following Wednesday, Melanie dropped by "to share the good news," she said. "We're going ahead with the business: Capitol Caps—a CAP-tivating purchase. Isn't that great?"

I found my mouth hanging open and forced it shut.

"Hugh Grudin is going in on the funding since he's not buying the knife. And"—she paused, then gave me her best "you can trust me" smile—"we're going to let you in on it too. Nick'll be by in a few minutes with paperwork. Really, Janine, it's the investment of a lifetime."

Need I report that I declined this rare opportunity?

I heard Nick and Melanie discussing my refusal as they left. "Oh well," Melanie said. "Janine is like that. She just doesn't get it." The last thing I heard was, "You know how every family has a black sheep? Ours is Janine."

Virginia V. Kidd brings a light touch to her writing. Her comedy plays for high schools, *Happily Ever Once Upon* and *Capricious Pearls,* are longtime sellers. "Murder, Self-Taught" is in *2013 Anthology: Capitol Crimes.* A professor emeritus in Communication Studies from CSUS, she co-authored *Cop Talk: Essential Communication Skills for Community Policing* with former Sacramento police chief Rick Braziel. She lives in midtown Sacramento with four stray cats who wandered in and took over.

CAPITOL CITY BLUES

NAN MAHON

It had rained in the predawn hours and the grass glistened with moisture. Early workers quick-stepped along the paths leading to the State Capitol. Joggers cut through the park, earbuds in their ears, listening to music as they ran.

California Highway Patrol Officer Rick James, on morning equestrian duty, urged his big bay mare closer for a better look. A man was in a sitting position on the floor of the California Vietnam Veterans Memorial, leaning back against the bronze statue of a weary combat soldier, helmet in hand. The man did not seem to be just another homeless drunk like so many who slept in Capitol Park every night. He wore an expensive blue suit with a red tie, and fine brown leather loafers with tassels.

Officer James dismounted, stooped over the man, and realized he was not drunk. The eyes and mouth were open, as if in surprise. The white shirt was blood-soaked from a bullet wound in his chest.

James reached in the saddlebag for a pair of sheer plastic gloves and put them on. He squatted beside the body, pulled back the suit jacket and found a wallet in the inside pocket. He leaned back on his heels and stared at the identification card for a minute before calling his sergeant over the microphone attached to his uniform shirt.

"It's Martin Mason," he said. "The assemblyman. Looks like he was murdered."

***

The pounding on the door became louder and more insistent. Startled out of a sound sleep, Amos sat up in bed, disoriented. Then he remembered that he was in a hotel room.

85

"Amos Richards. Sacramento City Police. Open up."

"OK, OK." Amos ran his hand over his face, struggling to get fully awake. He reached to the floor, found his jeans, and pulled them on. He picked up his shirt from the carpet, put it on without buttoning it, and went to open the door.

Two men in jeans and sport coats stood there. They moved the jackets back to show the badges attached to their belts next to holsters with nine-millimeter guns. "Detective Bentley and this is Detective Lopez. Can we come in?" said one.

"Sure." Amos stepped back from the door. He was still groggy and a little hungover.

Once inside, the detectives scanned the room. Amos looked with them at the almost empty bottle of vodka, the two glasses, his shoes and underwear tossed on the floor, and the remainder of a joint dropped in a third glass. Two guitar cases and an amplifier were in one corner. Lopez pushed open the bathroom door and looked in.

"You alone?" he asked.

"Yeah. Somethin' wrong?"

"Show me some identification."

Amos reached in his back pocket for his wallet. He had dropped his jeans in a hurry without removing anything from the pockets last night.

Bentley studied the driver's license Amos handed him. "Live in Baton Rouge? Why are you in Sacramento?"

"I'm a musician. I play guitar with Blind Buddy O'Brian. We have a gig here at the Memorial Auditorium."

"You must be a high-dollar band to afford the Hyatt Hotel. How long you been in town?"

"Just got here yesterday."

Bentley handed the license back to Amos. "Been partying a little?"

"Some, I guess." Amos ran a hand over his short, tight curls. "What's this about?"

"What did you do last night?"

Amos began to get concerned at the questions asked by two city cops. It was not the first time, as a light-skinned black musician, that he had been rousted. He lived in the Deep South. He knew better than to get defensive.

"I was at the Torch Club here. It's right across from the Auditorium," he said. "Got up and sat in with the band for a couple of songs. You can check with them."

"Good-looking guy like you don't have any trouble hooking up, I bet. You know a woman named Susan Mason? Hot blonde, about forty years old?" Bentley looked around the room again, his eyes resting on the vodka bottle and two glasses, one of them still partly full, lipstick trace on the rim. "She come back here with you? Do a little drinking and smoke a little weed?"

"Who? Susan what?" Amos said. "I don't know what you're talking about. I don't know any Susan."

"Talking about the woman who came up here with you last night. It's on the security camera. She stay here all night? What time did she leave?" Bentley asked the questions. Lopez stood just a few feet back, watching.

Amos realized he really didn't know when she had left. "I must have been asleep. I didn't hear her leave. Could have been anytime."

"She said she knows you from way back," said Bentley. "She said you and her husband got in a hassle last night outside the Torch Club. Said you threatened to kill him."

"What? Are you messing with me?" Amos couldn't believe what he was hearing. "I just met the woman last night at the bar. She said her name was Suzie, came up here and we partied a little, but that's it. I don't know her husband, never met him, didn't know she had one. You got the wrong guy here."

"Yeah? Well, he had a ticket to your show tonight in his wallet. Must've been a blues lover," Bentley said. "Put some shoes on. We're going to take you to the station and talk some more."

"You got it on the security camera. You know what time she left. You know I didn't."

"We're getting a copy of the tape now," Bentley said. "We'll see what we find."

87

"I have a performance tonight," Amos protested. "Can we do this tomorrow?"

"Put your shoes on," Bentley said.

***

Ivy was waiting for him in the courthouse lobby when Amos came out of the interrogation two hours later. She walked straight up to him and put her arms around him. He held her against him and felt the warmth of her affection. He wanted to stroke her hair, run his hands down her arms, and kiss her softly. But she was Buddy O'Brian's girl, not his.

"Thank you for coming," he said.

"I've been so worried ever since you called. What happened?"

"These sons-of-bitches think I committed a murder. It's just plain nuts."

"I know you, and I know this is some kind of mix-up. Do you need a lawyer?"

Ivy was not beautiful, just pretty like a million other women. Her light brown hair fell just past her shoulders, her lips were full, and her eyes were blue as a summer sky. The thing about Ivy was that she cared. She cared for everyone, and to Amos, that was a beautiful thing in itself. But, most of all, she cared for Buddy.

Buddy was visually impaired, seeing only lines and shadows, so the music world called him Blind Buddy. He was a moody, angry, talented musician. He cheated on Ivy sometimes and sometimes went on a drinking binge. But Ivy would not leave him. If asked why, she would say simply, "He needs me."

Right now, Amos felt that he needed her more.

"Buddy know?" Amos asked.

"Yes, I told him. He's worried."

"Worried I won't make the gig?"

"Amos, you know better than that." Ivy took his arm. "You must be hungry; I know they didn't give you anything to eat. Let's go back to the Hyatt. I'll buy you dinner and you can get cleaned up before the sound check."

"Yeah, I need a shower. Let me do that first and meet you in the hotel restaurant."

***

When Amos came down to the restaurant, he felt a stab of disappointment when he found Ivy was not alone. Sitting at a table with her was Strum, the bass guitar player, and Buddy.

Buddy's black Irish curls reached almost to his shirt collar and a small gold loop hung in his right ear. He wore dark glasses to protect his damaged eyes from the florescent lights and, even from across the room, anyone in the know could recognize that he was a blues musician. A seventy-pound black and tan German shepherd lay at his feet.

"What you got yourself into, man?" Strum asked as Amos took a seat beside him.

"They got me made for something I didn't do." A waiter came up to take Amos' order. He told him a steak, medium rare. He wanted to order a bourbon and water, but, like the other band members, he hesitated to drink around Buddy. Anything could set him off on one of those crazy binges.

"You OK to play tonight?" Buddy asked.

"I'll be fine. You won't have to carry me."

Buddy shrugged and took a bite of his club sandwich. "Ivy said she will help you find a lawyer. Wanta tell us what happened?"

"I was over in the place everyone says is the blues spot in town. Called the Torch Club, 'cross the street from the gig. Sat in with some of the locals and had a couple of drinks at the bar. This blonde chick comes on to me and pretty soon she wants to come up to my room."

Buddy looked up from his plate, waiting. Ivy took a drink of water. Strum cocked his head to one side.

"We partied a little. I fell asleep and I guess she left."

"So, what's the problem?" Strum asked.

"Somebody killed her husband," Amos said and waited while the waiter put a steak platter in front of him. "Problem is, her husband was a big-shot politician."

89

Strum, the oldest of the group, was tall and whip thin; his lined face was the shade of dark charcoal. He shook his head. "You always messing with some strange woman. Told you over and over that would jam you up someday."

"I don't go lookin'. She come on to me."

"You just too pretty for your own good. Get yourself a good woman like my Ruthie, or Buddy there with Ivy, she always got his back."

Amos looked over at Ivy. She was smiling, signing her name and room number to the bill.

"Time for the sound check," Buddy said. "You going over, Strum?"

"Yeah, I can handle it. Amos, you go on to your room and get some rest."

"That OK, Buddy?"

"Yeah, go on, we'll take care of it. Just show up on time." Buddy stood up and Ivy rose with him to take his arm. "Come on, Mojo," he said to the dog.

When the three of them were gone, Amos went into the hotel bar and ordered bourbon over ice.

A slender young man who looked to be in his early twenties with dark hair that fell onto his forehead, almost touching his rimless glasses, came in. He looked around the bar, then walked over and took the stool beside Amos.

"You the guitar player with Blind Buddy's Band?"

"Yeah. Amos Richards." Amos was in no mood for a fan, but he offered his hand, mostly out of habit.

The man ignored the gesture. "You're good-looking. I bet you don't have any problems with getting women, do you?"

"What? Are you crazy? Get out of here."

"All of them want to have sex with you, don't they?"

"Get the hell away from me." Amos gulped the rest of his drink, and then got up and walked away.

Amos went to his room, hoping to rest. He was dead tired. He sat on the edge of the bed and took off his shoes, but before he could lie down, there was a knock on the door. He sighed and walked across the room to open it.

The two men standing there were dressed in dark blue suits, white shirts, and striped ties. "Amos Richards?" one asked.

"Yeah."

"Investigators Bill Smith and Charlie Bushnell. We're with the California Bureau of Investigation," said one. "May we come in? Need to ask you a few questions."

Amos opened the door wider and stepped back. "I already talked with the police."

"That was the city, we are state investigators. An assemblyman was murdered, so we are involved now," said Smith. "We'd like to check out your belongings."

Amos shrugged. "Help yourself."

The two men looked around the room. Maid service had been there and cleaned up the glasses from the night before. They opened the dresser drawers and checked the closet. Then they took the two guitars from their cases and shook them upside down.

"You're looking for drugs, right?" Cops always thought black men had drugs.

"Assemblyman Mason may have been mixed up in narcotics trafficking," said Smith. "You know anything about that?"

"Because I'm a blues musician and we're all doing drugs? I just got into this town yesterday for a gig. I've never been here before and I didn't know the assemblyman." Amos felt the anger rising inside him. "I have to perform in a couple of hours, so just get out of here or arrest me."

"Look, Richards," Bushnell spoke up, "if this is about trafficking, whoever killed the assemblyman may have you in his sights, too. Watch yourself."

The men left, leaving the two guitars lying face down on the floor. Amos picked the instruments up and put them back in their cases. He sank onto the bed and put his hand over his eyes.

But sleep would not come, so he walked out of the hotel and onto the street, crossing over to the manicured lawn of the State Capitol. He followed the curving pathway until he reached the Vietnam Memorial. It was a serious and sad tribute to sacrifice and duty, only a small distance from the Capitol building.

Assemblyman Mason had worked and died on these grounds. It was twilight; workers had vanished from the premises and long shadows lay on the grass.

Maybe the two detectives were right that he could be in someone's crosshairs. Or maybe they were just trying to scare him. The whole thing had him a little spooked.

He went back to the Hyatt, got his guitars and amplifier, and caught a cab to the Memorial Auditorium. The other band members were on stage finishing the sound check when he got there.

"Where the hell you been?" Strum called to him.

Amos plugged in his amp and his guitar, a white National Resonator with a sheer metal plate across the body, and hit a few licks to be sure he was coming across clearly. Strum picked up his bass, while Franklin, the band's keyboard man, and Scott, the drummer, joined in. They did an old Muddy Waters tune, just warming up.

Amos drifted into that zone that musicians go to, that place where the music takes over and flows out through the instrument in their hands. Frustration, sorrow, and pure blues chords poured out in the strings of Amos' guitar. His body rocked with every note and his eyes closed, his fingers moving across the strings.

Stagehands and people wandering through the auditorium stopped to listen. Buddy O'Brian, with Ivy and Mojo beside him, stood at the edge of the curtain, moving his head slightly with each phrase. It was one of those moments that some artists call magic, the time when they find something they didn't really know was there and the art comes from some hidden place inside them.

A figure moved on the opposite side of the stage. Mojo growled. Then he began to bark. He was running across the stage just as the sound of a gunshot shattered the moment. Mojo leapt and brought down the gunman in one swift, powerful motion.

A bullet hit the middle of Amos' guitar and knocked him to the floor. He could feel the force of it as he went down, his arms flung out, the strap holding the guitar against him. He blacked out as his head and back hit the stage.

When Amos opened his eyes, Ivy was on her knees beside him, talking on her cell phone, saying please hurry. Franklin and Scott were holding someone down and Buddy was calling to Mojo to let him go. Amos recognized him as the young man in the bar.

Ivy had her hand on Amos' face, crooning, "It's all right baby, you're going to be all right."

Police came rushing in, pushing Franklin and Scott away from the gunman. Then the paramedics were there, squatting down by Amos, cutting the guitar strap so that the instrument fell away, tearing off his shirt and pressing something against his chest.

As they lifted him onto a gurney, Amos saw Buddy standing nearby, talking to a man, and sounding agitated. "Look, man, we'll go on tonight, or tomorrow night, or when you want us to. We can do it without the rhythm guitar."

"We're sold out and we open the doors in two hours," the man said. "We have a contract."

"I said we'd go on, you sorry bastard."

Amos saw Strum move next to Buddy and put a hand on his arm.

"Let us check on our man here, see if he is going to be alright," Strum said in that quiet, matter-of-fact way of his. "We'll be ready when the curtain goes up, if the cops say we can. We'll give you a good show."

The paramedic put a mask over Amos' nose and mouth, and he lost consciousness as he was lifted into an ambulance, with Ivy climbing in beside him. When he woke again, she was sitting in a chair next to the bed he was lying in.

"How do you feel?" she asked.

"Like someone dropped an amp on my chest."

"Doctor said the metal plate on your guitar saved you. You got a couple of busted ribs and you will be sore and bruised, but you will live to play the blues in another concert or two." She picked up a business card from the nightstand. "A Detective Bentley came by, said he would be back."

Amos reached out his hand. Maybe there was a chance she cared the way he did. "Thank you, baby, for being there for me."

She took his hand and squeezed it. "Buddy and I are your family, that's what a band is. We love you and we'll always be there for you."

He sighed and let that dream go.

***

The next morning, the doctor came in and told Amos what a lucky man he was and that he would be released as soon as they bandaged him up and ordered some pain pills for him. He was getting dressed when Bentley showed up.

"You're one lucky man, Richards."

"Believe me now?"

"Yes, we do. CBI is taking over now because they think Mason was dirty. They think he was helping move some drugs. As for the murder, that's a different case. The kid talked to us. The poor little fool was one of Mason's aides. Seems he and Mrs. Mason were involved. He said Mrs. Mason told him if he killed her husband they would be together. They set you up for her alibi."

"She say it was true?"

"Naw, she denied it. Got a lawyer."

"Goin' to let the kid take the fall?"

"We'll see. He keeps crying and saying she betrayed him, that she was just supposed to sit up. She wasn't supposed to have sex with you."

Amos searched his memory without finding warm skin or tangled limbs. "Funny thing," he said. "I was pretty wasted, but I don't believe she did. I passed out before we got to that."

Nan Mahon's characters are the less-conventional people, who by design or fate, live in a dangerous and edgy world; they are the different, the talented, and often the disenfranchised. Mahon draws her people from those she has met in her work as a journalist, a band agent, and music promoter. This story continues the characters from her novel, *Blind Buddy and Mojo's Blues Band*.

HOT TIME IN OLD TOWN

PATRICIA L. MORIN

I skimmed my copy of the *Sacramento Daily Register-Union,* December 7, 1894, yet again, and sipped the cold coffee as I sat at Fat City restaurant in Old Town, Sacramento. I was here to meet Amanda Leonard, acclaimed historical mystery novelist. She had posted a copy of the newspaper article on her blog and announced that Sacramento was the site of her next book.

The article from the *Sacramento Daily Register-Union* read: *Eugene Myerson, a resident of Sacramento, fell from a train and was run over by its cars near Swingle.* Amanda had researched Sacramento, Swingle, the old newspaper, and the Myerson family. Then she Googled historians in the area, and found me. When she called, she shared that she had received a letter threatening to "take her out" if she wrote her next historical mystery about the death of Eugene Myerson.

So there I sat waiting.

The restored 1876 legendary Pioneer Bar counter from Leadville, Colorado, caught my wandering eyes, and I also spotted the Johnnie Walker Black on the wooden shelves behind it.

Late. Did she talk to her publisher about the threat? I rubbed my hands on my blue jeans, inspected the neon-yellow check mark on my running sneakers, and thought about Johnnie, smooth-tasting, fast-acting Johnnie. I could hear the ice clink against the Scotch-filled glass, the light golden-brown liquid blending with the soda, and smell the nasal-clearing aroma. I sipped my coffee.

Why was I so anxious? All I had to do was help her fill in some of the historical blanks around Myerson and his life. My family, self included, had never left the area. The Sullivans served as politicians, police, lawyers, and even knew Indian chiefs. Many were teachers, like me, except I had my doctorate in history and taught at the University of California at Davis, a town about forty minutes south of Sacramento.

Was I in danger?

Through the door, a tall, slender woman walked. She scanned the room, set her eyes on me, my denim "Life is Better than Good" baseball cap that I use as an identifier, then the papers, and then back on me. She resembled the picture on the back flap of her last book, prettier, with sandy-blond, shoulder-length hair. But those piercing black eyes were just like my son's when my cop father came and took me away, drunk and loud and threatening my ex-wife. It was my first and only drunken rampage, but I will never forget my son's dark stare of disappointment.

I smiled, nodded, and stood. She returned the smile. I had to watch I didn't bubble over with facts about Sacramento and constantly interrupt her, one of my ex-wife's many complaints. I was the expert on the chronicles of California's history, especially Sacramento, named after the river of Holy Sacraments by Spanish cavalry officer Gabriel Moraga. Yep, I knew it all.

"Amanda Leonard?" I asked the comely lady.

"Rudy Sullivan, I presume?" She grinned as she extended her hand.

We shook, and she sat opposite me, placed her large handbag on the floor, then stared up at the plethora of varying stained glass-covered lights above us. "They're beautiful, and very different." Her lips parted slightly as she scrutinized each light shade, as if to say, "look at that ceiling, the stained glass!" She reminded me of how Alice must have reacted to her first sight of Wonderland. Light shone on her hair, and she had a few thin lines on her forehead that bunched together. According to her book cover, and my math, she was in her late thirties.

"Yes, that one," I said, pointing up, "is called the Purple Lady, and won the stained glass competition at the 1893 Chicago World's Fair. Can I buy you a drink?"

"No, water is fine with me, but I'll have a sandwich. Um, what's good?" She removed her navy blazer, which matched her navy slacks, and draped it on the back of the chair. Her multicolored plaid shirt brightened her complexion. No jewelry, not even a necklace or pin. Hmm ... she's not bad, I thought. Not married either.

I shrugged as I handed her the menu. "It's extensive," I said. "Been here many times." Then I added, "So sorry to hear about the threat. 'Take you out' is like old Mafia lingo."

She skimmed the menu and settled fast. Then kept her eyes on the menu as she said, "I get scared, then not scared. See, um, I don't know how serious to take it." Her eyes flitted to mine, then my ear, then my forehead. "Then I remind myself my book is fiction, and I just want some historical facts to make it feel real. I won't be using anybody's name, so why would I even be threatened? The case is a hundred and twenty-two years old."

As if on cue, the waiter scooted over, introduced himself, and took Amanda's order for a hamburger and water with lemon. I ordered fresh coffee and a turkey burger.

"So, Mr. Sullivan—"

"Call me Rudy. OK to call you Amanda?"

"Yes, of course." She spoke softly and had difficulty with eye contact. "You know who you look like?" She affixed her eyes momentarily on mine.

I laughed. "Yeah, most people say I look like Matt Damon, but with glasses—so I guess I'm a techie Matt Damon. My wife used to get so annoyed when people would say that. We're divorced." The last sentence raced out of my mouth before I could pull it back.

Shit!

"Well, you do look ... like Matt Damon ... in glasses." She stumbled for words, and then paused in thought. "I'm sorry I was late. I was admiring the fire station, Sac Engine #3, right around the corner, and lost track of the time. Organized in 1851, after the fire that destroyed many establishments in the city, and built in 1853 after the *great* fire. This town ... it had a lot of fires ... and floods. The hook and ladder of its day, um, so I guess they would say. Looks like Eugene Myerson was, well, he was a highly respected firefighter." She gazed at the lights, then studied the California Pacific Railroad building across the street. I wanted to tell her that the railroad building was built in 1865, eleven years before it was taken over by the Central Pacific Railroad, the railroad financially backed by the Big Four: Hopkins, Crocker, Huntington, and Stanford, in 1861, the same year as the American Civil War began. She probably already knows that, I thought.

Don't talk too much, I warned myself.

She scanned the stained glass lights again, then rested her eyes on me.

"Do you think someone is out to kill me? I mean, really?"

"I don't know. We'll have a better sense of that once we explore all the pieces. Did you call the police, or your publisher?"

"Not yet," she said, and slipped her hand into her handbag. She withdrew a few laminate-protected pages, probably dated over a hundred and twenty years ago. "I have here authentic pages from Charlotte's diary, Eugene's girlfriend."

My heart raced. Where did she ever find those treasures? Maybe she would sell them to me after she finished her research.

"Read this encounter she had with Eugene Myerson in the River City Saloon."

With heart still pounding, I read the passage, neatly written, from November, 15, 1894:

I met a most interesting man today in the River City Saloon as I waited for Aaron to finish collecting his taxes. His name is Eugene Myerson, and he has the widest blue eyes I've ever seen. He's a hook and ladder man, big and strong and handsome, not capricious in any manner. Delightful, though. Forthcoming, but with a humor that could not be thwarted. He sat right across from me as I was reading the Sacramento Daily Record-Union and offered to buy me a drink! I ordered a sarsaparilla. We spoke of the immigration problems, and the anti-Asian sentiment. He's one of those new Democrats.

By the time we finished our third drink, and Aaron walked in, I had feelings for Eugene, a strong, beautiful man who made me laugh. And, as you can imagine, I knew I couldn't, no wouldn't, see him again, me a married woman to Aaron Schiller!

"Wow!" I skimmed the document again. "Wow, this is incredible! Where did you get this?"

The meals arrived and Amanda stacked the pages to the side under the windowsill.

"At an auction. I go all the time. That's why I picked Sacramento." She looked at her plate. "Charlotte was born in 1860, so she was thirty-four," she continued, then inhaled the scent of the food, paused, inhaled again, then smiled. "I'm a foodie, and this smells wonderful."

Yep, Alice in Wonderland.

She sliced a piece off the burger and placed it in her mouth, as if tasting a hamburger for the very first time. "Good, too."

"Great," I answered. "Maybe you could write that Charlotte's husband murdered Eugene! She was married to the tax collector, a prestigious job in those days. Those men were often big and burly, able to defend themselves against robbers, and they often partnered with a Pinkerton agent, one who protected the stagecoaches carrying gold."

"Interesting," she said. "I'll use that. I wonder if Eugene went to Swingle alone."

Several long moments passed as she paused in thought. I asked, "Any more information?"

She jerked out of her reverie, and handed me another laminated page. The paragraph was short and dated November 21, 1894.

I fear the consequences of my passion, dear Diary. Eugene and I met again this day. My heart thumped. I don't know how else to describe my physical reaction. He breathed in my hair, near my ear, and I felt chills all the way down my corset. He kissed me for the first time. A longer kiss I have never experienced, and never from Aaron. Dear God, don't let Aaron suspect that my love has shifted.

"So there. Oh my God, this hamburger is the very best! It's juicy, warm, oozing with … flavor. I like it here. Do you?"

"Yes, this building was originally built around 1849 by Samuel Brennan as a general merchandise store—first store to be established."

"No, I meant Sacramento. I like Sacramento, and this hamburger."

"Oh, yes, me, too." I didn't know how to respond. I had never met someone who called themselves a foodie. I had read that she was an only child. Attended private schools and graduated from Sarah Lawrence College with a B.A. in English. Jogger, reader, loner, loved to eat out, and volunteered at Golden Retriever rescues. Lived with three rescues in Manhattan.

"Would you like to read this letter from Eugene to his father?" She handed me another letter. "Do you want to read it out loud? I don't want the food to get cold."

November 28, 1894: I must say I was told to keep my distance from a woman, Charlotte Schiller, who is collecting the taxes for her husband, Aaron Schiller. She is opinionated and has a bad temperament. She demands a proposal of accommodation from the chief. I will show constraint, and not prejudice her against us. The chief is resigned to answer her questions, but she is of very ill temperament. The chief explained that her husband's temperament is even worse.

"That's very interesting." She wiped her hands on her napkin. "Maybe they were arguing? There is a one-week difference from one note to the other. Who knows what could have happened between them. Maybe her husband, Aaron, found them out?"

"Or Eugene's wife? Were there any letters, or information, in reference to Aaron or Charlotte after that date?" I asked, completely captivated.

"Not that I found." She glanced up at me and smiled. Sweet. Girlish. Vulnerable. "I have a meeting with one of the grandchildren of the Schillers at two o'clock. I called and asked them if they knew about the letters. Told them I was being threatened. They said they didn't know anything about the letters, but would check with their family. The granddaughter called back."

My cell rang. Dad. "I'll be right back," I said as I left the table, then the restaurant. "Hey. What's up?"

"That's what I was going to ask you. How's it going? Your brother's across the street watching the building."

I gazed across the street and there he was, talking to a buggy owner, petting the horse. He waved and I nodded as I filled my dad in on the lunch.

"The Myersons? Schillers? They've been at each other's throats since way back, Rudy. Does she know that? In fact, Irv Schiller is running on the Republican ticket for city council. Interesting that this is coming up now."

"I didn't know Irv Schiller was a Republican. How did you know they were at each other's throats?"

"Myerson's a Democrat. Arguing about the immigration policies."

"God, does it ever change?"

"The question here is, does she know how it would impact the families if she uses this for her book? Watch out for her."

I clicked off and returned to my place at the table.

"Did anyone else call you to respond about your inquiries?" I asked, then smiled. For some reason, something about her attracted me. On the one hand, I wanted to pull her gently through this difficulty, speak softly, coddle her, and explore the history of Sacramento together. On the other hand, why would I invite her difficulties into my life? But my ex-wife's serious nature and logical mind bored me. She needed the pattern of her routine to ground her. I found Amanda's aloofness and food-loving nature refreshing. Fun.

"No, no one called me." She pulled her food even closer, took the last bite of the burger, chewed, and closed her eyes in a joyful expression. "Yum. This is yum."

Burgers eaten, and after a long lull in the conversation, I asked, "Did you ever read anything else from Eugene's point of view, his wife, or his family? More articles?"

"No." She polished off the fries covered with both ketchup and mustard, and pushed the plate away, waving both hands in front of her as if thwarting the temptation from the food. "Can't eat another fry." She wiped her mouth. "I didn't want to spend too much time researching him. I mean, I wanted to do more research on Sacramento and have questions to ask you about that. So, OK if I call you later in the month when I'm filling in the history?" Her eyes rested on mine while she spoke.

"Sure. This is very interesting." I had to ask, "Did you know that both the Myersons and the Schillers still have relatives here, and that Mr. Irv Schiller, a Republican, is running for city council?"

"Yes. Well, I knew both families had relatives here. *The Sacramento Bee* had many articles about the election and who was running for office. Do you want to come with me?"

"Yes, I do." I caught the waiter's eye and he came right over. "I'll take the bill."

I paid the bill, and Amanda thanked me, that sweet smile beaming at me.

***

I didn't know they still had uncomfortable, plastic-covered blue couches around anymore. Mrs. Schiller, a short, thin lady somewhere over eighty, showed us to her three-cushioned couch and offered us coffee, tea, or wine, while she carefully considered our bodies, faces, and I guessed, moods.

Amanda shook her head. I accepted the coffee, black.

Amanda studied the yellowing walls with photos of land and water scenes, and Mrs. Schiller moved toward her kitchen. Family photos crowded another light blue wall.

The glass circular dish on the scuffed coffee table held cellophane-covered peppermint candies and I grabbed one. Amanda headed to the photo wall. She studied each and every picture.

"Do you think her mother would have known about Aaron and Charlotte?"

"I would think so." I tilted my head back and forth in a maybe, maybe-not gesture. "I hope she can help you with the threatening letter."

Mrs. Schiller steadied her hand as she placed the coffee on the table. "How can I help you? I was so sorry to hear that you received a threat about writing this story! Have you any clues yet who may have sent it?"

I could smell it before I sipped the horrid coffee, instant, out of a jar, and in a teacup.

Amanda wrung her hands in a nervous gesture. "Not yet. I thought it might have to do with Mr. Schiller's election, and the possibility that, well, that, in your history, a man might have been pushed off the train by a Schiller." She paused and spaced out on the peppermint candies. She must do that when she is anxious.

"Did you know about Charlotte Schiller's feelings toward Eugene Myerson?" I asked. "She was your grandmother, is that correct?" I added, hoping Amanda would come back to us soon.

"Yes, she was. Amanda"—she caught Amanda's attention— "you spoke to my daughter-in-law on the phone, and she called me right away."

Amanda pulled out the laminated pages from her shoulder bag and handed them to Mrs. Schiller, accompanied by an uncertain smile. "Would you like to read these? I bought them at auction."

Mrs. Schiller stood. "I'll get my other glasses." She shuffled into the kitchen. "Looks like we'll find the answers here." The sunlight glared at me through the front window, the only light in this lifeless home. The room smelled of stale air, like a mausoleum.

Mrs. Schiller shuffled back to her seat and read. "So they did date!" Mrs. Schiller screeched. "I always suspected they dated! In her diary, pages were torn out. I wondered why. These are two of the pages! Oh my dear, you have proven what I have always suspected. You have found the missing pieces." Mrs. Schiller bolted over to the end table, opened the drawer, and withdrew an old, tattered, leather-bound book in a Ziploc bag.

"What pieces?" Amanda asked, squinting at Mrs. Schiller's back as if she didn't believe her. Amanda's mouth parted and her eyes widened at the sight of the diary.

"This is very exciting!" I exclaimed.

"Ah, well, yes," Amanda whispered as she leaned forward, eyes on the diary.

Mrs. Schiller then eased into a plastic-covered blue recliner opposite us, and removed the diary with care. She set it on the coffee table near the peppermints and opened it with her thumb and forefinger where "In Memoriam" funeral cards were placed.

She guarded the secrets, I thought, for all these years.

"Charlotte wrote this passage on December 3, 1984, and it's after Eugene's outrage."

Aaron's Pinkerton agent is following me. I don't know why. Does Aaron know? Does he not realize that I have found fit to avoid awkward meetings with the fire chief and his men, and am disposed not to interfere with his business partners? I will never bring him or our family embarrassment, nor would I make sport of, or call out, friends I hold most dear.

"I believe that is when Charlotte broke her ties with the friend she held most dear. If it was Eugene Myerson, the affair was a short, but strong one, I suspect."

Throughout history, love has captured and tortured mankind. Was it worth the joy? I didn't think so.

"Because, my dear Amanda," Mrs. Schiller said as she faced Amanda, "we are all Myersons as well as Schillers. Charlotte had a baby with Eugene Myerson. Before this time, she complained that Aaron had lost interest in her physically and she was jumping out of her corset. Later, it was discovered that Aaron Schiller was impotent." Mrs. Schiller smiled. "I have all your books, Amanda, placed on a special shelf. I love your stories. So creative! I did try to reach your mother before she passed away, but she wouldn't return my correspondences. She did not want to believe the truth, that is why she changed her name after your father's death. A conductor, paid off handsomely by your great-grandfather to avoid a scandal, saw Ginny Myerson, your mother's grandmother, push her husband off the train. Not much was made of people falling off the train in those days—it happened so often."

Amanda eyes bulged. "I want to leave now." She grabbed her pages and bag, and bolted out of the house.

I sat dumbfounded. "I don't think she knew she was a Schiller, nor did she think you would know who she was. You must have scoured the secrets from both family trees."

"Yes, I did, and for years. I found it fascinating, and now have the proof to place the final pieces in the puzzle."

"Clever. So *you* wrote the threatening note so Amanda would come look for you."

"Why, yes. I thought, when she wrote that creative piece in her blog about choosing Sacramento based on something she had found at an auction, that I needed to know what she'd found, what she knew, and most importantly, what she would do. Irv is running for city council, and who knows where he will go from there?"

I shook my head, and left. I pulled open the passenger door and found an angry Amanda. "Are you OK? Want me to drive?"

"Irv wrote the threat, right? Is that what you think?" She looked me straight in the eye.

"Mrs. Schiller wrote it." I repeated Mrs. Schiller's words. "Did you really find those laminated pages in an auction?"

Her eyes wandered around my face again, then settled on her lap. "No. In my mother's old trunk after she died. I decided to write a story that would incorporate it, and used my blog to see if I would get a response from someone here. I didn't expect such a threat. After all, it was my mother's grandmother who killed her husband. But I wanted to know more. I wanted to know the truth." She started the car and nibbled at her upper lip. "Now I don't know what to do."

"This is all very upsetting. But what you write will be very important to a lot of people. Let's go back to the restaurant, or take a walk." I wasn't certain how all this would work out, but I wanted her to stay. "You said you like it here. How about we go for some homemade ice cream? They have the best here, you know."

"Really?" She exhaled.

"A-huh."

"You're just saying that, right?"

"Nope, the absolute best ice cream." I crossed my heart.

She glanced at my shoes, then my shoulders, then my eyes. She smiled. "OK. A double scoop ... of vanilla." She paused in thought, as if she had made a decision about what to do. "With caramel."

I chuckled. It looked like Johnnie would have to wait. Again.

Patricia L. Morin MA, CSW, besides writing short stories, novels, and plays, has had four short-story collections published. Her first two short-story collections, *Mystery Montage* (2010) and *Crime Montage* (2012) were released by Top Publications Ltd., Dallas TX. Her short story "Homeless" was a Derringer and Anthony Award finalist, while "Pa and the Pigeon Man" was nominated for a Pushcart. Her third and fourth short-story collections, *Confetti* and *Deadly Illusions*, were released in 2014 and 2015. Please visit her website: www.patricialmorin.com

Not a Clue

Cherie O'Boyle

California State Assembly member Patricia Harper stared in puzzlement at the waxy brown object she'd found in the center of her desk that morning. The time was straight up six o'clock, and already she could hear Adam, her aide, bustling about in his office. Patricia herself was not bustling. She sat nursing a large Costa Rican blend, waiting for its magical powers to take effect. The opening of a new legislative session was always crazy busy, and she knew today would be no exception. She took another long sip, tried to slow and deepen her breathing, and poked at the object.

It had not been there when she left last night close to midnight. It might be a seedpod of some sort, or possibly a small art object. Perhaps a gift from a constituent. Or something Adam's toddler son had made in preschool?

Adam tapped lightly on the doorframe and entered, carrying an armload of proposed legislation. A stack of opened mail slid precariously on top, and he gripped a flat stationer's bag in his mouth. He dropped the pile of legislation on the corner of the desk, placed the mail beside it, and removed the bag from his mouth.

"Good morning! Here's the replacement ink cartridge for that pen you wanted for the bill signing. And here is your reading for today," he said without a hint of how ridiculous it was that she might possibly read all of that in one day. "The ones with blue Post-its on top are asking for your sponsorship. Top priority. The yellow Post-its are due for introduction this week. Those are top priority, too. And here is this morning's mail. I'm ready to go over that with you now, if you like. What's that thing?" He pointed at the brown object.

"I have no idea. I was hoping you would know. Someone left it on my desk last night."

Adam scrunched his lips, scowling. "It looks like an evil talisman. Anybody cast any spells on you lately?"

"What do you mean, 'lately'?"

Adam chuckled. Remembering a long-ago nature walk, he said, "It looks sort of like a castor bean. Those are the source of ricin, you know, that deadly toxin? Even a few grains of purified ricin can cause death in a matter of seconds."

Patricia quickly dropped the object into the shallow dish containing three bright Susan B. Anthony dollars on the credenza and withdrew her hand. She should have Adam do some research on that.

"Where's the rest of the pen?" He gestured at the shiny silver base of the fountain pen where they'd left it disassembled and carefully laid out the night before. The cap was missing. They both inspected the desk, under papers, and beside books. Adam even got down on the floor and felt around the carpet. The silver cap of the handsome pen was nowhere to be found.

"It's a mystery," Adam concluded. He collected the remaining parts of the pen and popped them into the bag. He would attach the new cartridge and reassemble the pen in time for the signing the following day.

"We'll just have to hope it turns up," Patricia agreed, reaching for the new stack of reading. The top item sported a hot pink Post-it.

"Oh, that's James Tyler's bill to protect feedlot operators from prosecution for animal cruelty. He wants, but doesn't expect, your sponsorship. After the end-run he did on you over the domestic violence funding bill I don't think you want to help him out with this one."

"Yes, you're right. I wouldn't support that bill in any case. You know, the real mystery is why anyone would want this job. Last year the California Legislature passed over a thousand bills. I probably read four or five times that many."

"If you want to lighten the workload, you should get yourself elected to Congress. They only passed a hundred and twenty bills last year."

"No, thank you! There's enough backstabbing here. I don't need to join that madhouse!"

***

Two hours later, Patricia stood to stretch. The pile had dropped by at least half an inch. Some progress. Not enough. She turned to look out the glass wall behind her, framing one of the Capitol's enclosed atria filled with greenery. Absently, she picked up the brown object and rolled it over in her fingers, examining its whorls and patterns. Definitely some sort of a seedpod, but why had someone left it on her desk? Could Adam be right? Was someone sending her a message? She put it down again. Probably she should go wash her hands.

On her return trip from the ladies' room, a bellow from inside James Tyler's office stopped her in the hallway. That guy was always mad about something. Apparently, he'd just discovered the governor had vetoed Tyler's bill to eliminate special funding for veterans' disability programs.

Patricia settled herself in for another hour or so of reading before the steady stream of morning meetings with lobbyists began. Everyone wanted something. As the office fell quiet once more, Patricia became aware of a faint but repetitive thumping sound. It seemed to come from the wall her office shared with James Tyler's. Sort of like James was gently kicking the wall. Patricia found the thump remotely threatening. She tried to concentrate on her reading and sometime later the sound ceased.

***

Dark came early that January afternoon, especially in Patricia's office, the only outside light coming from two stories above, where the atrium opened to the sky. Patricia's desk chair faced away from the window so that her visitors could have the view of the atrium gardens. There were no window blinds, since no one except gardeners ever entered the atrium. Even so, Patricia could feel the back of her neck prickling as the darkness drew closer. She shifted two or three times, then got up and moved to a guest chair. She was still clearly visible from the atrium, and couldn't decide if she felt better staring at the blackened sheet of glass. Close to eight o'clock she loaded up her briefcase and left the office in search of a quiet dinner.

***

Patricia did not notice the two-inch round mushroom in the shallow dish next to the brown seedpod until mid-morning the following day. Although she was no expert at identifying mushroom species, this one looked deadly. She liked mushrooms, but she didn't eat them unless she found them in a bin at the supermarket, and even some of those looked iffy. She rolled this one over with a tentative finger, noticing as she did so that two of the Susan B. Anthony dollars were missing. That was odd, and somewhat creepy.

She pressed the intercom and asked her staff to put down whatever they were doing and come into her office. If this was a joke, it wasn't funny.

Each one of them solemnly affirmed their innocence, and Patricia believed them. That only deepened the mystery. The door to the office suite was securely locked every evening. There were no other entrance doors. The front office was never left vacant during the day. Although building maintenance had keys to all the offices, they rarely entered without notice. All office waste was emptied before the staff left each evening. It was not possible for anyone to have entered the office and left these items on Patricia's desk.

Dismissing her staff, she picked up the phone and called Tom in Special Services, the closest the Capitol building had to a security office. When she had him on the line, she explained her concern that someone was entering her office at night, and asked for his advice.

Within an hour, Tom was at her door, followed closely by her aide, Adam. Tom unrolled a blueprint showing the wing of the Capitol building in which they now sat, and spread it across the desk. Patricia placed the heavy, shallow dish, now containing the seedpod, the mushroom, and one silver dollar, in a corner to prevent the blueprint from rolling up.

"We have coverage of the door to your suite from two cameras mounted here"—Tom pointed—"and here. Only, this second one stopped functioning several weeks ago. There's no money to repair it until the next budget year. I've reviewed ten hours of video from each of the past two nights, ten p.m. to eight a.m. Except for you and Adam leaving and arriving at various ungodly hours, no one has entered this office during those times from the direction where we have video.

"There is also no access from the atrium. You can see here"—Tom pointed again—"this access door into the atrium around on this other hallway, and over here"—he pointed to the opposite side of the atrium—"is the door used by gardeners to do maintenance inside the atrium. Again, no access into your office."

The three of them sat back and looked at each other.

Tom shifted uncomfortably. "Any chance this could be a stalker situation?" he asked.

"A stalker! Who would be stalking me? Anyway, how would I know if I had a stalker?"

"Calm down," Tom said. "I'm not saying anyone is stalking you. I'm just trying to think through the possibilities. Who's leaving these items here, and why? Most people know if they have a stalker."

Patricia felt her face go warm as she shook her head. During the legislative sessions, she had no time for a personal life. She knew she had annoyed a succession of potential dating partners by being too distracted and too busy to pay them sufficient attention. Leaving small, potentially toxic objects in her office seemed an outlandish way to protest.

Tom picked up the seedpod and rolled it in his palm, pursing his lips. "Ask me, I think someone's playing tricks on you. Still, we don't want any unauthorized persons getting into your office." He cut a low glance in Adam's direction, and Patricia could see what Tom was suggesting.

"No one on my staff left these items here. I've already spoken to them. We're all as puzzled as you."

"OK then. Best I can do is ask the California Highway Patrol to send an officer through this vicinity once or twice tonight. Since the budget cuts, highway patrol is the only security force we have in the Capitol."

Patricia turned to look again through the glass and into the atrium, feeling suddenly vulnerable, both for herself and for her staff.

"I'll ask for a patrol inside the atrium too, just in case somebody's getting in there. You can see, though, no one can get into the office from out there." He stood and inspected the large single pane of glass. Like all windows in the Capitol building, this one did not open.

He turned to the dish and poked at the mushroom. "What are these things anyway?"

"The brown one, I don't know. A castor bean?" Patricia sent Adam a questioning look. "And the mushroom, possibly a poisonous toadstool?"

"You guys piss anyone off?"

Adam gave a hollow laugh. "Every day. You know how it is around here."

Patricia caught Tom's gaze. "Listen, Tom, I may be overreacting, but I'm feeling threatened. If leaving these items is a message to me, well, castor beans contain the deadly toxin ricin. Adam says even a small amount of ricin can kill. And if this is a toadstool, those can be deadly also. I don't know if this is about anything specific, anything someone is really angry about and is threatening me or my staff, but I'm taking this seriously."

Tom said he understood, reiterated about the extra patrol, and left. Patricia and Adam went back to work. An hour later, they gathered up the remains of the commemorative pen and the paperwork, then hurried to a committee room for the signing ceremony.

Returning from a late lunch with the co-sponsors of her animal rights bill, Patricia heard the unmistakable sounds of James Tyler in the midst of another temper tantrum. The loud "thwack" of several books or a pile of papers hitting the floor in his office reverberated into the hallway. Patricia scurried into her own office.

Almost as soon as she settled behind her desk, the same insistent thumping she'd heard the day before began again. It sounded as though James was throwing a rubber ball against his office wall, except the thumping was too rapid. Heaving an annoyed sigh, Patricia headed to Tyler's office, intending to ask him to stop.

"Oh, I'm sorry, ma'am," Tyler's secretary said when she got there. "Assemblyman Tyler left the office about ten minutes ago."

Confused, Patricia explained about the thumping and asked if she and the secretary could step into Tyler's office to listen. From there, they could hear the thumping clearly, coming from the wall adjoining Patricia's office. By the time she returned to her own office the baffling noise had stopped.

Darkness had fallen when Adam and Patricia concluded their daily debriefing and planning for the following day. Adam stood, anxious to get home to his young family, then froze with a yelp.

"Hey!" He pointed out the glass behind Patricia. "There's someone moving out there!" Patricia whirled in her chair, but could see nothing in the direction Adam pointed. It was too dark, the office lights reflecting against the glass.

At the same time, the voice of Patricia's secretary called out from her desk in the front office. "Sir! Please let me tell her you're here!" Before she could finish her sentence, James Tyler burst through Patricia's doorway.

"Did you see him?" he asked in excitement. "He was right there." Tyler waved to the left side of the atrium. "I swear, I saw someone moving out there. Did you see him?"

"I'll call Special Services," Adam said, picking up the phone.

"Yeah, you do that," Tyler snorted. "They'll be here in twenty minutes. Big help." He stepped to the glass wall and peered out, cupping his hands around his eyes while Adam completed his phone call.

Tyler turned to face them. "I'm telling you, there was some creep out there. And here we sit, not allowed to bring guns into the office. No way to defend ourselves. I'm telling you, I'm introducing a bill tomorrow. This 'no guns' policy is ridiculous! And I am bringing my gun tomorrow!"

"If you bring a gun into the Capitol building, James, that is not going to end well, I can promise you that."

Adam's eyes were big. "And what are you planning to do, shoot right through the glass?"

Tyler mumbled something about "lily-livered liberals," and marched out of the office.

Patricia met Adam's eyes. "Don't you think whoever you saw was probably the officer Tom said he would send out there to patrol?"

"I saw something moving, but I didn't see who. The reflection on the glass is too bright to see much. But it's only five thirty. Why would anyone be patrolling out there already?"

***

The bustling of the rest of the staff preparing to go home penetrated Patricia's consciousness a short time later. That would leave her alone in the well-lighted office, clearly visible to anyone lurking in the darkened courtyard. A shiver ran down her spine. She stood and began packing as much reading as she could carry into her briefcase. She'd finish the evening's work in the two-room apartment where she resided during legislative sessions.

"Ma'am?" One of the office interns stood in Patricia's doorway, her bulky coat zipped to her chin.

"Yes, Kate. What can I do for you?"

"I only wanted to tell you, I think that brown thing you found is a redwood tree seed or cone."

Patricia picked up the object in question and held it out to the young woman. "This thing?"

"Yes. There's a bunch of them on the ground near the bicycle racks on the north side of the building. I saw them when I came in this morning. And there's a whole grove of trees there. *Sequoia sempervirens*, coast redwoods. I think that's what it is."

"So, not dangerous at all," Patricia said.

"No, unless you wonder how it got in here. That would be the real mystery."

"Yes, well, thank you very much, Kate. I will certainly sleep better tonight knowing this is only a redwood seed."

***

But she didn't. Believing the objects were intended to deliver a frightening message was a mystery for professionals to solve. Knowing at least one of the objects was easily found and of no particular significance made it seem like a puzzle she should be able to figure out herself.

***

Patricia arrived at her office door just before six the next morning. She had crept along the hallway from the usual direction, intently listening for the sounds of others moving at that hour. She placed her cardboard cup of morning brew on the floor next to the door, and leaned the briefcase against the wall. Still wearing her deerskin gloves, she slipped the key silently into the lock and turned. The click it made was almost inaudible. The door swung open to reveal the darkened office. One tiny red light glowed steadily on a computer monitor, and, like a string of miniature holiday lights, five dots shone from the modem under one of the desks. Other than those, the darkness was nearly complete.

She left her coffee and briefcase where they were and stepped inside, silently, her footsteps muffled by the carpet. She stopped to listen, mindful of how someone could emerge from the short hallway in front of her at any moment. She realized that sneaking in like this could get her seriously hurt if someone was waiting for her, hiding in the office. On the other hand, Adam should arrive any minute, so she probably wouldn't have time to bleed to death.

She stepped into the faint rectangle that was the entrance to the short hall leading to her office and stopped again. Illumination from outside threw faint light into the hallway. At least she would see him coming if someone tried to rush her there. Behind her, two women just arriving for work laughed and called out to each other in the main hallway.

When that sound faded, she listened again. Nothing. She took the few steps that put her into her office doorway. Unless someone was hiding behind the desk, or in the shadows beside the file cabinet, no one was in the office. Still, she could hear someone in the dark, not breathing, but … trembling. Moving slowly, she raised her arm, found the light switch, and pressed. Fluorescents buzzed to life overhead.

A quick glance around the office revealed nothing out of place. The top of her desk, left clean the night before, was still empty. Patricia shifted her gaze to the credenza and the small dish resting there. It contained one redwood cone, one now slightly shriveled mushroom, and nothing else. The last dollar was gone. And something else, but she couldn't say what.

Patricia lowered herself into a guest chair without shifting her eyes and continued to stare. Then she saw it, nestled between two binders on the top of the credenza. The tiniest twitch of the pink-brown nose brought Patricia's eyes into focus. She could only see half of the furry, cinnamon-colored body, about one-third as tall as the binder beside it. The creature held its plump head, decorated with compact, round ears and long black whiskers, as still as a statue. It looked steadily back at Patricia with bright black eyes. Its miniature hands were clasped primly in front of the buff fur on its breast. Neither of them moved for several long seconds, simply examining one another in wonder. Then, perhaps having decided Patricia was only part of the furniture, the creature reached up to adjust the

Susan B. Anthony-sized lump in its cheek, stroked its whiskers, and turned to disappear behind the back of the credenza.

***

"From your description and its behavior, your visitor is most likely a *neotoma fuscipes*, a dusky-footed woodrat, or what is sometimes referred to as a 'packrat',," explained Maria, the technician from the wildlife rescue organization. "Probably a young female, judging from the size. We'll know better after we catch her."

"And what happens to her after that?" Patricia asked. "I called you instead of anyone else here because I didn't want her poisoned or caught in some horrible trap."

"We'll catch her, give her a quick vet check, and then decide if she can be safely released into a vacant territory in the foothills. If we can't find a place where we're confident she'll survive, we may keep her at the center as part of our educational exhibit."

"And that thumping I heard in the wall?" Patricia asked. "Was that the woodrat?"

"Yes," Maria said. "Woodrats do that with their back feet when they're alarmed. She's probably scared living this close to humans."

Both Adam and Patricia shook their heads in wonder. "Wow," said Patricia, "she's been through a lot in her young life."

"Yes, she has," agreed Maria. "We'll try to take good care of her from here." She stood and gestured out the window at her assistant setting up and baiting the humane trap inside the atrium.

"Is it true that packrats trade their own treasures for our shiny objects?" Patricia asked.

This garnered a smile from Maria. "The cap of your pen and the Susan B. Anthony dollars, you mean? It does seem like she was leaving you payment for those, doesn't it? It's more likely she was already carrying the redwood cone when she found your pen, and had to drop the cone in order to carry the pen.

Same thing with the dollars. But without being able to ask her, we really don't know. Possibly she was generously paying you with her treasures in exchange for yours."

Cherie O'Boyle is the award-winning author of the Estela Nogales mystery series. *Fire at Will's*, *Iced Tee*, and *Missing Mom* are humorous whodunnits set in the fictional village of Arroyo Loco in the central coastal mountains of California. O'Boyle is Professor Emerita of Psychology at California State University, San Marcos. You can read about her books and contact the author at www.cherieoboyle.com

IT'S WRITTEN IN THE STARS

KAREN PHILLIPS

Their horses' breaths formed misty clouds in the early-morning air as they rode in silence, watchful and vigilant, past the building that housed the senate, legislature, and governor of California.

On her patrol horse, Officer Rosa Ramirez looked up above the portico at the bare-breasted female warrior sitting atop a white steed, spear in hand. Rosa sent a silent request to watch over and protect her while on duty. She thought of the warrior as her guardian angel.

The two mounted officers moved into the forty-acre grounds of Capitol Park. Tule fog had settled into the lowlands of Sacramento, where trees and statuary formed an eerie landscape. As they stepped out from under the overhanging branches of a towering redwood tree, Rosa's horse hesitated and his ears twitched. A large bundle lay on the parkway in front of them.

"Easy there," Rosa said, patting her horse on the neck. The Belgian draft shifted his huge feet, metal shoes clattering on pavement.

"What's wrong with Sherm?" Officer Thompson asked, as his own horse moved under saddle. "He acts like he's never seen a homeless person before."

"Not one sleeping in the middle of the road," Rosa said.

Both officers reined their horses back a few feet.

Rosa's nose wrinkled at the strong scent of urine.

"Pee-yew. Get a whiff of that," Thompson said.

Rosa kicked her boots out of the stirrups and landed firmly on the ground. "Here," she said, handing the reins to Thompson. "Take Sherman upwind. I'll check it out."

Thompson circled the horses around and up onto the grass. "Hey," said Thompson, raising his voice, "that coat looks like the one the Homeless Hero wears."

Please, no, Rosa thought. *Not on my watch.*

She stood over the body. "Wake up," she said. Nothing. No reaction. Nada.

Something about the stillness of the body made her pull her gun. She slowly circled the body, noticing the coat's distinctive black-and-white herringbone pattern and black collar. The man who everyone called the Homeless Hero wore a herringbone coat.

Her weapon out, she stepped closer, stuck the toe of one boot to a shoulder, and pushed.

"Dios mio!" she cried out as the head rolled back, separating from the rest of the body.

Sherman nickered. A shadow moved, then ran off through the trees.

Rosa dropped to one knee. "Stop or I'll shoot!"

Thompson threw Sherman's reins to the ground and spurred his horse in pursuit.

Rosa stood and slowly looked around, peering into the gloom. Every dark shape looked suspicious. The only sounds were her own breathing and her heart pounding. She vaguely became aware of other sounds—car tires on wet pavement, the hiss of brakes of a commuter bus, a distant emergency siren. Convinced there was no immediate threat, she called the incident in.

"Hold your fire, Ramirez," Thompson said, emerging from the trees. "I'm back." Rosa noticed his lack of usual bravado. His horse tossed his head and stomped his feet as if in mutual frustration.

"No luck?"

"Bastard got away."

"You sure it was a man?" Rosa asked.

"By the shape of him and the way he ran, I'd say ninety percent sure."

"It's not the Hero," Rosa said, staring down at the dead man's face.

"Who is it, then?"

She cleared her throat. "It's Walker." Rosa holstered her gun. "You know, the homeless guy who walks laps around the park and picks up trash?"

"Why the hell is he wearing Hero's coat?" Thompson said. "Doesn't make sense."

"It never does," Rosa said. *But I'll figure it out,* she silently promised the dead man.

***

The fog slowly cleared and the park filled with light. The gold of the Capitol dome shone brightly. Police cars formed a blockade as a small crowd gathered. State workers mingled with the homeless. Rosa scanned their faces, wondering if the killer was among them.

Sergeant Maldrum stood next to the coroner, taking photos with his cell phone. He shook his head as if in disgust, then turned to Rosa, his eyes sweeping over her petite form. "At first you thought it was who, again?"

"The Homeless Hero. It's his coat."

"Homeless Hero?" said Maldrum, a smirk in his voice.

Rosa opened her mouth, but Maldrum raised a finger. "Don't tell me," he said, passing by so close she could smell his aftershave. "Your latest conquest after you crossed me off the list?"

Anger flared through Rosa's veins, the heat of it burning like a shot of tequila. She followed Maldrum to a large magnolia tree. "Come on, Sarge. He's been in the news trying to help the homeless."

"You ask me," Maldrum said, "whoever took this dude out is the *real* hero."

Rosa glared at her boss. "I can't believe you said that."

Maldrum spat on the ground. "You're dismissed, Officer Ramirez. Get on your pony and ride. You and Thompson have reports to file."

127

***

That night Rosa sat on her sofa, feet up on the coffee table, watching news while eating a salad. She popped a crouton in her mouth and looked down at her dog.

"Chiquita, you want one?"

The little Jack Russell terrier sat trembling with anticipation.

Rosa tossed a crouton in the air. Chiquita jumped, catching the treat in one bite.

"Good girl!"

The commercials were over and the news was back on. A reporter stood in front of the Capitol steps; behind her, a crowd of people milled about, holding signs.

"Early this morning a homeless man was brutally slain. The victim's name was Greg Martin," the reporter said. "Martin was wearing the familiar coat of the Homeless Hero." She turned to a homeless man standing next to her. His gray hair and full beard hid most of his face. He wore a faded, olive-colored coat.

"Most of us know this man as the Homeless Hero," she said.

The crowd behind her broke out in cheers.

The reporter flashed white teeth at the camera. "Today we will find out the Hero's real identity." She paused for effect. "The Hero is none other than actor Sergio Storm, who has taken Sacramento by storm," she said, winking at the man next to her, "in his efforts to help the homeless."

The man scowled.

"Sergio, can you remove some of your makeup so the viewers can see your true identity?" The reporter reached for his face as if to pull away a mask. Sergio grabbed her hand.

"Don't you dare touch me!" he said.

The reporter gasped and Sergio released his grip. He smiled at the camera. He grabbed his nose and pulled.

Rosa dropped her fork in surprise as she watched the actor's nose come completely off to reveal his real, patrician nose—his trademark feature.

Sergio cleared his throat. "I have chosen to disguise myself and live among the homeless in order to understand, firsthand, their plight. I appeal to the governor, and the people of California, to vote yes on the homeless bill. I ask all of you to follow me and help the homeless!" He punched the air with a fist. "Let's do this!"

The crowd roared, pushing their signs into the camera view. Rosa read, "Help the Homeless," "Vote Yes for Homeless Rights," and "Stop the Crazy Train!"

The reporter smiled again. "You are also here to do research for your next movie?"

"Yes, that is true," Sergio said. "My next movie is about a rich man who loses everything and becomes homeless. This experience is critical to my role."

"I notice you're not wearing the herringbone coat we all recognize you in. The victim was wearing a herringbone coat. Was it yours?"

Sergio's expression was a studied mix of grief and anger. "That's right. Greg was one of my friends. He wanted my coat, so I traded with him." Sergio pulled at the lapels. "This is his coat and I'm proud to wear it. I will always think of him. His death will not be forgotten."

"The burning question I have, Sergio, is, was Greg's killer really after you?"

The camera switched to a close-up of Sergio's face. Fury flashed in his dark eyes. "Mark my words," he growled, "whoever you are, you do not scare me. That includes all you who support the governor's 'Crazy Train'! The homeless *will* be heard!"

Rosa sat mesmerized, her fork frozen in midair. Could Sergio's support of the homeless bill derail the governor's high-speed rail project—the Crazy Train? Sure seemed a good way to make enemies. The sound of the cell phone interrupted her thoughts. She answered the familiar ringtone, "Hola, Mami. Que pasa?"

"Papi and I are worried about you, Rosita."

Rosa sighed. "You saw the news."

"Si, Rosita. You know how your father feels, so he asked me to call."

Rosa took her dishes into the kitchen. She looked out the window at the stars and recognized the constellation Pegasus, the winged horse. Fond memories came flooding back as Rosa recalled nights in the fields, far away from city lights, when her father taught her astronomy and the stories behind the constellations.

"Rosita? Are you there?"

"Yes, I'm here," Rosa said. She wished her father would respect her decision to be a police officer. She had graduated top of her class in the academy, but only her mother attended the swearing-in.

"Listen, Rosita, por favor. The news said a homeless man was killed in front of the Capitol—where you work! And now someone is trying to kill that movie star pretending to be a homeless person? You don't want to get mixed up with those people."

"It's my job to protect them," said Rosa. "And to find the killer."

"I'm handing the phone to your father. You tell him that."

Now her dad was on the phone. He had to be worried, as he hadn't talked to her since she announced her decision to join law enforcement.

"I tell you, Rosa, you should have been a doctor, a lawyer— a wife, a mother! For God's sakes," said her father, "anything but a policewoman!"

Rosa groaned. "It's nice to talk to you too, Papi," she said, trying to lighten the mood.

"You think it's funny to worry about your daughter every day she is out on the streets with a killer? Dios mio, Rosita! It would help if there were a man in your life."

"I know you want to protect me, Papi, but I'm not a little girl anymore."

"Es verdad," he said, choking back a sob. "I love you."

***

A few minutes later Chiquita growled, then ran out of the kitchen barking.

"Chiquita!" Rosa said, following her.

Someone knocked on the door.

Chiquita barked again, her hackles up.

"Chiquita! Silencio!" Rosa said. She looked through the peephole and saw Sergeant Maldrum.

She opened the door. Chiquita growled. "What's up?" Rosa asked.

"Sorry to show up unannounced," Maldrum said.

Chiquita continued to growl as he walked in.

"Once a bitch always a bitch," he said, then chuckled. "The dog, I mean."

"What do you want?"

"I won't stay long. I wanted to come by and tell you in person."

Rosa's hand jumped to cover her trembling lips. "What? Has something happened to Sherman? Or Thompson?"

"What? No, no. They're both fine." Maldrum pulled a plastic bag from his coat. "A note was found under a rock at the crime scene. Inside of the chalk outline."

Rosa saw a piece of paper inside the bag. "You came to tell me about some note?"

Chiquita whimpered.

Maldrum handed Rosa the bag. She read, "Tell that mounted patrol officer to stay away or she could get hurt."

Rosa gasped. "Ridiculous! You think this is intended for me?"

Maldrum put his arm around her. "Babe, this case has brought back feelings I thought were long buried. When I saw you today, I saw a woman full of passion. It reminded me how good we were together."

Rosa stood still, waiting.

"I have to say, this case lit a fire under your ass," he said, squeezing her shoulders for emphasis. "And, honey, that got me *very* excited."

Rosa spun away from his grasp and faced him.

"You brought this note pretending to be concerned for my welfare?" she said, furious with rage. "Just so you could make a pass at me?"

Maldrum backed away, hands up. "Hey, take it easy. You're treating me like I'm some criminal."

Rosa opened the door. "You make me wonder if *you* wrote that note. I think you should go now."

***

The next morning, Rosa rubbed Sherman's velvety soft neck and thought about the note Maldrum showed her. The handwriting was familiar.

"How long have you known Sarge?" she asked Thompson.

"We worked together in Los Angeles, before I moved here," Thompson said, surprised. "Why?"

Rosa shrugged. "I heard a rumor he killed a homeless person in L.A., but I never had the guts to ask him about it."

"Yeah, that's why he had to leave the L.A. police department."

"You think he's got something against homeless people, Joe?"

"I hope not," he said. "Now I've got a question for you. I heard you and Sarge had a thing going. Is that true?"

Rosa shook her head. "That's old news."

"Hey, it's fine with me," he said. "Just asking."

"That was before he became our boss," Rosa said. "Anyway, it didn't work out."

"Oh, yeah? What happened?"

"He was like Dr. Jekyll and Mr. Hyde. One minute nice, then the next minute mean."

Thompson adjusted the girth strap of his saddle and prepared to mount. "I can see that about him. Anyway, good thing you moved on, right? Hey, did you see the news?"

"Yeah," she said, then laughed. "I can't believe Sergio Storm, here in Sacramento, posing as a homeless person. Is that for real?"

Thompson smiled. "It's like we've been cast in his next movie and don't know it."

Rosa sat up on Sherman's back. "Enough talk. Ready to ride?"

Before Thompson could answer, she kicked the horse into a lope.

"Hey," he yelled, "wait up!"

Pedestrians stopped to watch the two gentle giants running through the trees.

When they reached the steps on the north side, Rosa pulled Sherman to a stop. Thompson reined in next to her, his horse prancing in place.

"I really hate it when you do that," he said.

"That big grin on your face says otherwise."

Both officers turned when a group of schoolchildren walked up to them.

"Hey, can we pet your horse?"

"What's the name of your horse, lady?"

"Are you a policeman?"

The air was full of questions.

Rosa told them her horse was named Sherman because he was built like a tank. They giggled and the bravest of them reached their hands out to pet the horses, who bent their heads so the little ones could reach.

After the teachers led the kids into the building, the officers continued their patrol, heading over toward the California Vietnam Veterans Memorial, where a few homeless people sat in the sun.

Rosa dismounted and approached an older woman sitting on a bench. The woman eyed her nervously and as soon as Rosa was within a few feet she bolted. There was something about the woman that was familiar, but Rosa shrugged it off.

She turned to an older man nearby, and recognized Sergio Storm behind the makeup.

He looked up at her, shielding his eyes from the sun.

"Excuse me, sir," said Rosa, pretending not to know him. "I'm looking for information regarding the death of Greg Martin. Did you know him?"

Sergio fingered the bottom of his jacket with worn gloves. "I knew Greg. You gonna find out who killed him?"

"Yes, I am," said Rosa, handing him a business card. "If you think of anything that can help, please contact me."

"You be careful, lady," he said.

She walked over to a woman pulling a cart full of bottles and cans.

"Ma'am?" Rosa said.

The woman stopped. "What do you want?"

"Did you know Greg Martin, the man who was killed?"

"He was knifed. Right?"

Rosa maintained her composure. The news of how Greg died had not been released. "What makes you say that?"

The homeless woman looked around, and pulled at her thick sweater. "I know because it almost happened to me, right after Greg died, but that lady scared him off."

"What lady?" Rosa asked.

"The one who ran off when you got here," she said, then laughed. "She saved my life."

Rosa wrote the woman's name down and looked back at where Sherman waited for her. She walked over to where she had lost sight of the woman who fled.

"Nice day," said a man half-hidden on a park bench in the shadows.

"Oh," said Rosa, startled. "I didn't see you. Did you happen to see an older homeless woman run by?"

"She went thataway, miss." He stuck a thumb, indicating the direction. "I gotta tell you, though—that ain't no woman. She's one of them cross-dressers."

As she walked back to her horse, Rosa tried to shake off a feeling of dread. Was the killer dressing as a homeless woman?

***

When Rosa got home that evening the apartment seemed smaller, as if the walls were closing in on her. Even Chiquita couldn't lift her mood.

She slung her purse onto the coffee table and fell into the sofa. She closed her eyes. A knock on the door startled her.

"Rosa? It's Peggy."

Rosa opened the door for the landlady.

"Hi, honey," Peggy said. "I don't mean to disturb you, but when I was out walking Chiquita a homeless man stopped me and asked me to give you this."

Peggy gave her a small piece of white paper.

"What did the homeless man look like?" Rosa asked.

Peggy shrugged. "They all look alike to me."

With a shaky hand, Rosa unfolded the note. "You could be next if you don't stay away!" The lettering was similar to the note Maldrum showed her—it was familiar, but she couldn't place it.

"Peggy, I need to take this in as evidence. Did anyone touch it other than you?"

"No—no," she stammered. "Just me. Did I do something wrong?"

Rosa put her hand on Peggy's arm. "You did fine. Thank you very much."

She closed the door and leaned against it. *Breathe,* she told herself. *Remain calm.* She visualized the warrior woman atop the Capitol and heard her speak, "You are a fierce warrior. Together we will fight this evil man."

***

The next day, Rosa discussed an idea with Thompson.

"I'll dress like a homeless woman," said Rosa. "Make myself a target to lure the killer out."

"I don't like it," Thompson said. "Do you think I'd let you put yourself in danger?"

Rosa rolled her eyes. "I already have one overly concerned father. I don't need two."

"OK. OK."

"Besides, you got a better idea?"

"Yeah. I'll be the one to dress up as the homeless woman," he said.

Rosa shook her head. "Gotta admit, I am enjoying the visual," she said.

"He won't go for it," Thompson said.

"But I have to try," countered Rosa. She got out her phone and called Sarge.

"You got a plan? Let's hear it," Maldrum said. "I don't want the governor complaining that we aren't doing our job."

Rosa explained her idea.

"Way to be proactive, Officer Ramirez," Maldrum said.

Rosa gave Thompson a thumbs-up.

"However, the answer is no."

Rosa put her thumb down.

"On to Plan B," said Thompson, once Rosa told him that Maldrum had nixed her idea.

They rode through the park, stopping to question people about the murder. As the day wore on, the two officers split up.

***

As Rosa passed under a large oak tree, she suddenly was knocked off Sherman's back. She landed on the ground, the wind knocked out of her. She gasped for air and tried to get up, but someone jumped onto her back and tried to pull her helmet off. Rosa gagged as the neck strap cut into her windpipe, choking her. She grabbed at the chin strap and pushed the release button. Her helmet came loose and went flying to the side. Her assailant yanked at her hair, forcing her head back, exposing her neck. Rosa saw the sharp edge of a knife and screamed.

Up ahead, a gray-haired homeless woman ran toward them.

"Stop!" the old woman yelled.

The woman jumped over Rosa's head, sending her assailant sprawling to the ground. The knife skittered under a nearby azalea bush.

Rosa rolled over and got to her knees. She squeezed her eyes open and shut, and focused on the scene in front of her. The old woman lay on top of a masked man.

"Quick!" the woman shouted. "Cuff him!"

Rosa scrambled over to help, ripped the handcuffs out, and clamped them down on the masked man's wrists.

The homeless woman stood up, gasping for breath, and pulled her wig off.

Rosa cried out in disbelief. "Papi?"

"I just wanted to protect you," Rosa's dad said, his face full of emotion. "I couldn't live with myself if you got hurt."

"Dios mio, Papi! You're the one who wrote the notes!"

Her dad nodded. "Yes. I was only trying to scare you away."

Just then Thompson rode up, and Sherman whinnied in greeting.

Rosa bent down and pulled the ski mask off the man in handcuffs.

Sergio Storm glared back at her, spitting out bits of grass and mud. Without his makeup, wig, and facial hair, he looked pale and gaunt.

Rosa stared at his scalp, where a patch of hair was missing, revealing a jagged red scar.

"What happened to you?" she asked.

"Greg stole my coat, then scalped me!" Sergio screamed. "Homeless people are pigs!" he spat, a genuine look of disgust on his face. "I can't believe I let my agent talk me into this!" He raked his hands through his hair, then rubbed them on his pants. "I'll never get clean! I feel like my skin is crawling with vermin!"

Rosa stared, alarmed at the depth of his revulsion. *He must be a germophobe,* she thought.

"It was self-defense!" he said, eyes brimming with tears. "You must believe me."

"Rosa," said her dad.

"Yes, Papi?" Rosa said, breaking her gaze from the dramatic scene.

"You are the real hero."

Karen Phillips was born in Oakland, grew up in Martinez and attended Cal Poly State University, majoring in Applied Art & Design. While embarking on her writing career, she works full-time as a graphic artist in state service. The department where she works is located next to the State Capitol in Sacramento. She often enjoys walking around the park where mounted police patrol the grounds and became her inspiration for "It's Written in the Stars."

NOSE TO NOOSE

CLARE F. PRICE

Nose work can be exhausting. Hobbs is sprinting down the trail with me twenty feet behind, trying to keep hold of the tracking line. How he can move that fast with his nose glued to the ground is a mystery to me. We're in uncharted territory, having long since left the carefully prepared track I'd laid hours before. I have no idea where we are headed, but I trust his nose. Above all, I trust his nose.

We run through the thick manzanitas. His Sheltie coat is impervious to the brush. Maybe I should remind him I'm wearing shorts. A quick right turn. Hobbs stops short. His nose is pointed skyward. Nostrils flared. He's air scenting. Turning his head right, left. Nose to the ground. We're off again. A twist in the trail toward that ancient live oak.

I smell it before I see it. The sick, sweet odor of decay. Hobbs sniffs the trunk of the tree and turns to look at me. His nose has taken him as far as it can. He's too short to reach the feet. Human forensics is not my expertise, but it's clear from the purple toes and black soles that lividity has set in. He's been hanging there for a while. At least a day, maybe more. Flies have gathered in the eyes, the corners of his mouth, settled on the protruding purple tongue.

I pull out my cell phone and call 911.

***

"They said you found the body." She glared at me, stabbing her black-enameled fingernail on my desk like a knife blade. She'd charged into my office moments earlier, declared herself to be Tiffany Bui, tossed her Louis Vuitton handbag in my guest chair, gave her tight Elizabeth and James skirt a tug, and leaned over my desk. The late October sun highlighted her high cheekbones, giving her face the haughty appearance I sensed came naturally to her. Somebody's princess. No doubt about it.

The opposite of me: strawberry blond, gray-eyed Kate McCleery. I'm a Texan by birth, forensic scientist through education, amateur dog trainer with passion. The jeans and T-shirt covering my five-foot-seven, 115-pound frame were, as usual, hidden by a white lab coat.

"The police said you've helped them solve crimes," Tiffany accused.

"We do. The lab does, I mean."

I quickly detailed the role the Veterinary Forensics Laboratory at the University of California Davis played in solving crimes in which an animal was a victim, the perpetrator, or even a witness. My specialty was genetic DNA testing.

"I'm not sure how I can help you." I sent an inquiring look in her direction.

"Jack was my fiancé. They say he committed suicide. But he didn't. I want you to help me prove it."

"I'm sorry for your loss, but I don't see how I can help you."

"You found the body." Her voice edged up a notch. I guess she thought finding the body made me responsible. I needed to dissuade her of that idea fast.

"I was just out there working my dog. It's a police matter. Unless they request our help, we don't get involved."

Her almond eyes locked on mine. Her set jaw loosened as the anger she'd stormed in with evaporated.

"How would you feel if your fiancé were murdered and you didn't know who did it or why?" she asked, sinking into the chair beside my desk.

"Lost," I acknowledged.

Hobbs pressed his nose under her hand. A trained therapy dog, his desire to comfort was ingrained. Her fingers moved mechanically over his silky head.

Too much for me. The trouble was I knew exactly how she felt. My fiancé, Ryan Niven, was dead, too, killed in combat in Afghanistan. But I knew who and why. That's when I realized, against my better judgment, that I had to help her—or at least try.

***

Hobbs jumped into the front seat of my Chevy Silverado dressed for the investigation in his blue-and-black service vest. Hobbs is a sable Shetland sheepdog, affectionately called "Crazy Ears," because he's got one tipped ear and one pricked ear. At seventeen inches, he's considered oversized for the show ring, but he's perfect for me.

I climbed in, gunned the engine, and headed toward the natural first step in our quest—the Sacramento County Coroner's office, where my friend and colleague, Mia Lopez, the county medical examiner, would be waiting for us.

I'd already learned that Jack Turner was a legislative aide to Assemblyman Adam Cochran. Brilliant and cocky, with a relentless determination and a politician's deft style, Jack had experienced a meteoric rise among the Capitol staffers.

"So, you ruled the death a suicide," I said as we entered Mia's office. I took a seat on the institutional gray metal chair, as Hobbs dropped down beside me. Mia slid behind her desk. She faced me, arms crossed. This was not the bubbly brunette with an infectious laugh I knew so well.

"Why are you doing this, Kate?"

Shocked, I stammered, "Because I found the body."

Mia's eyes narrowed, expression grim. "This was a high-profile case. It's closed. There's no point in your getting involved."

"Jack's fiancée came to see me."

"She's trouble. Do you know who her father is?"

"No idea."

"Hung Bui."

Aha, I thought. That's whose princess she is. Hung Bui owned the Imperial Palace chain of upscale Asian restaurants. The flagship, Emerald Palace, was directly across from the Capitol building.

"She's been making accusations up and down the Capitol." Mia's tone softened. "We're friends. I don't want to see you get caught in the middle."

"Her fiancé was killed. She wants to know the who and the why. I think she deserves that."

Mia held my gaze for a minute longer, then pulled up the file so we could review the x-rays. I saw the inverted V bruise that indicated self-strangulation, the small bleeding sites on the lips, inside the mouth, on the eyelids. She walked me through the photos. There were no marks of intense struggle as would accompany a ligature strangulation. It looked like suicide to me, too.

"What about the missing shoes?" I asked.

Mia shrugged. "The guy was wearing a nice suit. Probably an expensive pair of wingtips. Great find for a homeless person. He didn't have a watch or ID on him either."

I agreed in principle. Everything she said made sense and, on the surface, fit the facts. Still, I couldn't get the picture of Tiffany's anguished face out of my head. I was hoping Mia would let me run my own tests.

"Can I take these?" I nodded toward the photographs. "And a clothing sample."

Mia gave me an inquiring look but she didn't object, probably because of the many cases we had solved together. Evidence bag in hand, Hobbs and I were on our way.

***

Hobbs stood at attention as the Capitol security guard went over him with the wand. We were running late for our ten o'clock appointment. I hadn't counted on such long lines at security. Cleared, we proceeded through the rotunda and entered the rabbit warren of hallways, stairs, and cubbyhole offices to arrive, slightly out of breath, at Cochran's office suite.

A bespectacled, dark-haired man who resembled an aging Harry Potter ushered us into the office. "Apologies. Assemblyman Cochran's been called away. I'm Simon Wicket, his aide. May I help you? Jack and I shared the legislative duties here."

"What was Jack working on?"

"The biggie was AB 1437, the Internet Fantasy Sports Game Protection Act."

"What's that for?"

"We want to protect players from the Internet sharks out there."

"Sounds like a good idea to me."

"Jack was getting some serious opposition from some of the fantasy game operators about the new licensing and state tax board requirements."

"What kind of opposition?"

Simon shrugged. "The usual. Lobbyists. Campaign donors. Nothing he couldn't handle."

I nodded. "Did Jack have any problems, work or personal? Problems maybe he thought he'd never solve?"

"Are you kidding? He was on track to run for the senator's seat when he retires next year. He just got engaged. He was riding the wave."

"Then why do you think he committed suicide?"

Simon thrust his hands inside his pockets. "I don't know. We got a full briefing. Everything pointed to suicide. I guess you never really know a person."

"Is there someone else I should talk to who might be able to tell me more about Jack's state of mind?"

"The only one I can think of is Ana Nguyen, VIP hostess out at the Gun Lake Casino. Jack spent a ton of time there, trying to get them to support the bill."

***

Ana Nguyen, a petite, raven-haired girl with a body that would melt ice, met us at the casino entrance later that afternoon. "Oh, what a beautiful dog," she exclaimed.

Hobbs responded with his most engaging canine grin. As we walked through the cavernous space to her office, Ana pointed out the high-limit gaming room currently occupied by two players and a card dealer with bulging muscles better suited to bodybuilding than dealing.

"So, you and Jack worked together?" I asked.

Her small, round face lit up, then darkened. "We did. Jack was lots of fun. I really miss him."

I nodded in empathy. "Were you making progress on the bill?"

"Bill?" She looked confused.

"Assembly Bill 1437, Internet Fantasy Sports. I was told Jack was working with the casino on the language."

"I have no idea what you're talking about. Jack was one of our VIP high-stakes poker players. When we were together, we sure weren't working on any bills." She giggled.

"I see. How was Jack doing? Winning a lot?"

"Usually. But he'd had a bad streak lately. Then last week he came in, paid his tab in full, and it was back to business as usual."

"That doesn't sound like someone who'd commit suicide, do you think? Newly engaged, out of debt." I agreed with Tiffany and Simon. This sure didn't spell suicide.

"Jack was engaged?" Her face turned bright red and she bit her lower lip.

"Yes. His fiancée asked me to look into his death."

She paused at her office door. "Well, he was quite a catch. Is there anything else?"

"No. Thank you for your time." She motioned for security. A uniformed officer marched us back through the casino with the kind of precision that reminded me of the classic perp walk. Which surprised me until he leaned down and whispered, "Wouldn't be asking too many questions about Jack Turner if I were you. He has friends here."

***

Unnerved from my encounter with the guard, I exited through the double doors into the bright sunlight, pulling on my sunglasses. Beside me, Hobbs kept glancing up, a worried look on his face. He could feel my tension through the leash.

I took a deep breath, tried to relax, more for his sake than mine, and started toward my truck. My phone vibrated in my back pocket. I glanced down and saw it was Lee. Of course he would call today. The second anniversary of Ryan's death.

"Hi, Lee."

The casino doors whooshed open. The security team exited. The one who'd walked me out paused, gave me a hard stare. I drew a sharp breath. They moved on.

"What's going on?" Lee demanded. A cop's gut now linked with a reporter's nose for news, Lee's instincts were almost as good as Hobbs'.

"Just a sec." I stepped over to the truck and let Hobbs and myself in.

"Kate. Are you there?" Lee's voice echoed through the speaker.

I looked down at his face. Astute hazel-green eyes, a knowing half smile, a strong, reassuring presence even on a flat digital screen. Lee Pritchard, Ryan's Army commander and best friend, had walked with me through the darkest days of shock and loneliness and of tragic loss: funeral, folded flag, desolate sister and parents. Though grieving himself, he held us all together. And he stayed in touch these last two years, available yet never obtrusive.

"Kate! Can you hear me?"

"Yes, I'm here." Hobbs barked his welcome too.

"Tell me what's going on."

"I found a dead body in Mather Field and now I'm hunting the killer."

"With a test tube in the lab, I hope."

"Not entirely."

"Could you fill me in?"

So I did. About the body, his identity, the ruling of suicide, the distraught fiancée's tearful plea. He grunted at that. I wrapped up with the potential gambling problem and my run-in with casino security.

"I'm coming up."

145

"You don't cover major crimes," I retorted. Lee was the top investigative reporter for Zenith, an online business and technology news site.

"But we cover politics. See you soon."

***

A little after five o'clock, I slid into the booth at Tilly's American Diner just as Lee was scooping up the last bite of a mammoth platter of fish and chips. He'd made record time driving up from Palo Alto. Lee glanced up as the waitress placed a cup of steaming hot coffee in front of me and refilled Lee's. A searching look. Eyebrows raised in question.

"How are you doing?" he asked.

He got a bright smile in return. "Fine," I insisted, trying to ignore the shadow of Ryan that Lee always brought with him. It wasn't his fault.

I shook my head at the waitress's poised pencil and took a small sip of the bitter coffee.

"It just hits me sometimes."

He nodded, feeling it too. Like I was now, when Lee's reassuring presence turned suffocating. He'd only been here a few minutes and I wanted him gone. A thousand miles away. So I could finally bury Ryan and the memories, once and for all. I hated myself when I felt that way.

"But it's getting easier."

"Good." He pushed an errant curl of sandy brown hair off his forehead and pulled a well-thumbed notebook out of his jeans pocket.

"I did some digging into our boy Jack's finances. He was in debt up to his hip boots. Maxed out on credit cards, second mortgage on the house. Pretty much on the skids. Then about two weeks ago he got $300,000 dropped into his savings account," Lee continued, flipping pages. "How do you figure that?"

"He was a gambler. Maybe he won big. Ana told me he just paid a big tab at the casino."

"It's possible." Lee didn't look convinced. White-collar crime was his forte. He had a hard time believing in luck when criminality would do.

"We'll know more as soon as we find out where the money came from. I've got some calls out," he added.

Lee paid the check and we walked out to the parking lot to separate trucks, but headed in the same direction. I'd told him to cancel the room he'd booked at the Best Western. He could stay with me. I hoped he would be OK on the couch. The spare bedroom was still stuffed with unpacked boxes from my recent move.

***

Lee tossed his green duffel in the corner of the living room and scanned my new digs. At just under a thousand square feet, two bedrooms and a bath, it was more cottage than house, but it was all mine. I was going minimalist with the new space to start. While I'd brought my rickety apartment tables and chairs to the eat-in kitchen, I'd splurged on a sleek modern mulberry sofa. It crunched with that new furniture sound as Lee dropped into the cushions. Hobbs jumped up beside him, reminding me I needed to sheet that sofa before it turned white and brown with shed hair and muddy dog prints. Lee picked up the framed photo on the side table of Lee, Ryan, and me posed beneath El Capitan.

"That was a good trip." The expression on his face was frozen halfway between a smile and a grimace.

"The best," I agreed. And the last, I didn't need to add. Ryan had been killed a month later. "I'm taking Hobbs for a walk. Coming?"

"You bet."

He popped off the sofa. I grabbed Hobbs' leash and we headed out the door.

As we reached the sidewalk, I glanced over and noticed a brown sedan parked across the street. "That's odd. I'm sure I've seen that car before."

Lee followed my gaze. "Where and when?"

147

"Outside the lab a couple of days ago and earlier today when we left the restaurant."

"I'll check it out. You stay here."

"Not happening."

As we started across the street, the driver looked up, gunned the engine, and yanked the car away from the curb at full tilt. Lee took up the chase for a few yards. Panting, he rejoined us.

"Got a partial plate. Gonna call it in." Lee spent three years with the Santa Clara PD before changing careers. He'd have no trouble getting it run quickly.

His phone rang just as we entered the house. "Belongs to Piedmont Security." He ran his hand through his brown hair, matted with sweat. "Now all we have to do is find out who hired them."

"Yeah, good luck with that."

With an enigmatic smile, he replied, "No problem. Zenith has a dozen hackers on the payroll."

Lee's hackers were back with answers in less than an hour with the news that Piedmont had been hired at one time or another by Assemblyman Cochran, Gun Lake Casino, and Hung Bui, Tiffany's father. Oh, the power of technology.

***

The next morning Lee took off to visit Assemblyman Cochran while I agreed to meet Tiffany at Temple Coffee near Arden. I spotted Tiffany at a two-top, grabbed my double shot cappuccino, and joined her.

"Any news?" she asked. I noticed puffy lines around her eyes. Grief had settled in. It made me more determined to help her find some peace.

"Just bits and pieces. I need to ask, how did your father feel about Jack?"

"Cautious at first. Jack wasn't Asian and he was a Democrat. That was hard for Dad to swallow. But once we got engaged, things were different. We had dinner a couple of weeks before…"

She swirled her latte. Tasted it, turned to me. "They were laughing, joking. It was such a relief because Jack had been so stressed the week before."

"He was almost $300,000 in debt. Maybe the kind of debt that could drive someone to suicide?" I mused.

A violent shake of her head. "No. I told you. No!" She slammed her cup on the table. The haughty princess had reemerged.

"I agree, Tiffany, because those debts were paid. Any idea where Jack could have gotten that kind of money? Maybe a loan from your father?"

She laughed. "No way. His favorite quote was, 'Neither a borrower nor a lender be.' He lived by it."

***

I took the back roads home to Davis, opening the windows to let the crisp fall air fill the truck with its scents and sounds. Hobbs' nose was going crazy.

Halfway there, I heard a pop and felt the thump, thump, thump of a flat tire.

"Crap," I muttered. I was crouched down peering under the truck bed for the spare when I heard a voice behind me.

"Need some help?"

I stood and gave him the once-over. Cargo shorts, plaid shirt over a UCD T-shirt, twinkling blue eyes, and enough muscles to do the job.

"Sure. Thanks." I turned back to the truck. "The spare's down—"

He grabbed me by the shoulders and jacked me against the tailgate too fast for me get a kick in. I felt a prick through my cotton shirt and against my rib cage. I struggled. He increased the pressure. It wouldn't take much more to thrust the blade up and into my ribs.

"Aaagh!" he screamed. Hobbs was on him. Teeth bared, my brave little Sheltie leapt up and grabbed his hand. The knife skidded past me. Hobbs had caught his sleeve. My assailant ripped his arm free and started running, Hobbs in pursuit.

149

"Hobbs. Come!" I yelled. He stopped, turned, and trotted back to me with his trophy, a swatch of plaid shirt. I ignored the trickle of blood down my side, grabbed an evidence kit from the cab, and carefully sealed our little piece of evidence. Then, though I loathed the idea of being the damsel in distress, I called Lee.

He changed the tire, patched my surface wound, and declared, "Until we figure this out, I'm sticking to you like glue."

"I don't need a bodyguard. I've got Hobbs." I gave him an affectionate hug. He was getting steak tonight.

Lee stood resolute. "Ryan would never forgive me if I let anything happen to you."

I didn't think Ryan was in a position to do much forgiving. But I didn't argue. I knew Lee really meant he would never forgive himself. He was good at that.

I handed Lee the bagged swatch. "Take this to Mia. Hopefully, she can ID him."

***

Hobbs and I returned to the lab. While Hobbs settled into his cuddle bed in my office, my scientific side kept repeating the old saw: when in doubt, retest. I moved to a testing table, pulled down the evidence bag Mia had given me, and methodically went through all the forensics. Nothing added up. The x-rays still showed a clean neck break that typified suicide without a struggle. But the photos showed some bruising around the collarbone I hadn't noticed before. Finally, I pulled Jack's suit pants from the bag and performed a microscopic analysis. That's when I found it: minute traces of cow dung on the hem of the pants.

My lab has one of the largest cattle DNA registries in the United States. Most of the locals register their cattle with us to prevent theft. A few computer clicks later I knew who owned the cattle and where Jack had been before he died.

I picked up the phone to call Lee just as his call came in.

"Got an ID on your perp." His excitement crackled through the phone. "His name is Earl Redman. He's a dealer at the Gun Lake Casino. I'm heading out with the Sacramento County sheriff to pay a call on Mr. Redman now."

"I've got something too. Cow dung on Jack's pants. And those cows are owned by Hung Bui."

***

I sat across from Tiffany in the blinding white of her lavish living room. She sat rigid and dry-eyed as I told her the whole story.

"Your father was a partner in one of the largest Fantasy Football sites on the Internet. If Jack's bill passed, it would have cost them millions. He paid Jack $100,000 to kill the bill. But Jack double-crossed him and fast-tracked the bill because the casino paid him twice as much. But that wasn't your father's only motive." My voice dropped.

"Jack was having an affair with Ana Nguyen. That pushed your father over the line. Not the money. You. His princess."

Her chin wobbled and for the first time I saw a tear drop.

"Redman was supposed to rig up an accident, but Jack showed up at the ranch to demand more money and recognized Redman and the casino guard. They panicked and improvised. Redman had been an EMT in Vegas so he knew how to stage a suicide."

"Thank you. It's good to know the truth." Tiffany stood up. "I need to get some rest."

"Of course." I stood, gave her a hug, and wished her farewell. She was queen of the empire now. I hoped it would help her keep her sanity the way my job was helping me keep mine.

I hurried home. Hobbs and I were going tracking in the morning and we weren't planning on finding any more dead bodies.

Clare F. Price used her life experience as a tech journalist and software industry executive to craft her first novel, *Web of Betrayal*, the fictionalized account of one of the Internet's first cyber terrorists, published in June 2014. She continues her writing pattern of real life informing fiction in her new mystery series about a canine CSI team, Kate McCleery and her Sheltie Hobbs. Look for Book 1 of the series coming June 2017.

GIMME A BREAK

R. G. ROSE

Have you ever had that feeling, just knowing, that things were going to change real soon? Mine was so strong that when my mom put yet another community college flyer in my face, I told her about it. The big break I'd been waiting for was so close that I could feel it, almost smell it and touch it.

"Yes." She was nodding like a bobblehead. "We're all intuitive. You need to pay attention to those feelings."

A few days later Mom told me about her talk with her friend, Leann. "She did your horoscope and said you were absolutely correct about a change coming. She got a very strong feeling about the letter A."

"Are you going to tell me the 'A' means American River College?"

"No! That's what I thought, too, but Leann said it was definitely a female with the initial A."

"Uh, Mom, did you by any chance mention to Leann that I was dating a girl named Ashley?" I was skeptical of most of my mom's friends.

"Well, maybe," Mom admitted. "I might have, you know, when I was giving her your backstory to help with a more accurate reading."

"Thanks, but I'd be more impressed if she told me something I didn't already know."

"There's more. Leann said you need to be very careful. Things aren't what they seem. She can probably give you more details, but you should meet with her yourself. And I believe sooner would be better than later."

"OK, Mom, sure. But now I need to get to work." I gave her a peck on the cheek, grabbed my keys, and headed to Cuppa

Better Brew on Fair Oaks Boulevard. It was a blazing hot Sacramento summer, but this coffee place still did a brisk business. It brought in some pastries and pretty decent cookies, and it kept busy with people from surrounding office buildings.

I'd been working there maybe five or six months and I should've been made assistant manager, but the manager had it in for me because a few dollars had gone missing on a couple of my shifts. He was one of those wussy guys who was scared of illegal terminations, so he never came out and accused me of anything, but I knew what he was thinking. Then Mike, a pimply faced kid who'd only been there two months, got a promotion and raise instead of me. The place was making big money selling its overpriced latte cappuccino frappe mocha crap. The triple-digit heat just made people want it on ice.

I was the one who remembered all the self-important customers' names and what they ordered every time they came in. That really reinforced their sense of superiority and made them happy. They loved me and I was good for business, so I didn't feel guilty about a little extra money finding its way into my pocket. Besides, I was only there temporarily. I'd had some bad luck and needed a job to put some cash together.

I was dating Ashley, an eighteen-year-old hot little blonde who just graduated from Rio Americana High School. Cuppa Better Brew was her first job and she was all happy and enthusiastic. She'd been accepted at Stanford for having some 4.0 grade point average since kindergarten, belonging to a bunch of the right clubs, and playing tennis and volleyball.

I tried to act more impressed than I really was. The truth is, I'm just as smart as her or any other college-bound kid. I could have shown any of them up if I'd been able to catch a break like they did. It didn't matter. I never wanted to go to Stanford anyway. I was keeping my eyes open, because I knew that my luck would change soon.

In the meantime, I was working part-time at the coffee shop to get enough money to move out of my mom's house. It was a stupid job, but Ashley's smile and optimism made it bearable. And Mike had the hots for her, but she liked me, which anyone could see made him really mad. How could some little pipsqueak Cuppa Better Brew assistant manager, who couldn't even buy beer, compete with a twenty-three-year-old, good-looking (so I've been told), experienced guy with something of a bad-boy reputation?

Ashley and I had been going together for almost the whole summer and mostly we just hung out. Her dad worked as an assemblyman at the State Capitol and her mom was some kind of insurance executive. Sometimes they'd give us tickets people had given them and I'd take Ashley to see a concert at Sleep Train Amphitheatre. Other times, it would be a gift card for that expensive sushi place downtown. I'd always be really polite and effusively grateful to her parents, but I knew her dad didn't approve of her dating someone my age who worked in a minimum wage dead-end job. He was one of those typical political types: a short guy, always wearing an expensive suit and shiny shoes, always on the phone about this bond measure or that bill. Ashley worked at the same place as me, but that didn't matter. He was sure to let everyone know his daughter was going to the same university that Chelsea Clinton had attended.

I got along with her mom, though. I'm six-foot-two with a broad-shouldered frame and dark hair and, as I mentioned before, considered good-looking. Ashley's mom loved it when I turned on the charm.

Ashley hated both of her parents. It's true they were both fake and dishonest and way too fixated on appearances. On the other hand, they had their reasons for being that way. Her dad was planning on running for senator and her mom was a high-powered executive. It went with their jobs. They were well-connected and knew all the right people. That's why things fell into place for them and why Ashley got to be a little princess going to Stanford.

But Ashley was mad at them because they wouldn't let her do what she wanted to do, which was move to LA and study acting. She'd been in, well, "starred" was her word, a few stupid high school plays. Oh, excuse me, "productions," and everyone told her she had "star quality." She refused to work in either her mom's or dad's offices. She chose Cuppa Better Brew herself. It didn't pay much, but she said finding me made up for it.

The last week before Ashley left for college, I thought my big break had fallen into my lap. We went to dinner at Cheesecake Factory with a group of her uber-boring ex-high school friends. Seriously, I thought my mind was going to explode from listening to their insipid yakking. But then my eyes focused on the pearl-and-diamond necklace she was wearing. I'd never seen it before and I leaned in close and asked her where she got it.

Ashley blushed a little and put her hand to her throat and said, "My grandmother gave it to me for graduation. Do you like it?"

Everyone commented on how lovely it was, but I knew they hadn't seen what I'd seen. Later, after I was able to separate her from the herd and get her alone in the car, I brought up the necklace again.

"It really is lovely and I know something about fine jewelry. I used to work in a high-end jewelry store." OK, technically it was a pawn shop in Reno, but I'd learned a lot about recognizing quality and estimating values. I also knew about moving valuable pieces.

Ashley smiled and I could see how pleased she was. "It was Nana's. She has a lot of old pieces. Some are even antique pieces from her mom. I've especially loved this necklace since I was a little girl. Nana always said I could have it when I was grown up."

"Wow, she sounds really great. Does she live here in Sacramento?"

"Oh, sure. She lives pretty close to the coffee shop actually."

"Maybe I could meet her sometime. Do you think she'd like to show me her collection? I have a professional interest in antique jewelry. Plus, it would be nice to meet her."

"Well, I love her and we're really close, but I don't know if she'd want to show them to you," she said. And then she continued in that animated high-speed voice that drove me crazy. "My Nana's been a widow for a long time and she lives with her cats. My little brother thinks she's creepy, but my mom and I visit her. Poor Nana. She's really going to miss me when I'm away. I'll miss her, too, and her sweet little kitties. I'm feeding them this week while Nana's gone on an Alaskan cruise with her golf buddies. Jason! You aren't listening!"

"What? Yes, I am. I was just thinking, though, that you won't want to take something this valuable with you." I gently fingered the pearls at her throat. "It's way too precious. You wouldn't want anything to happen to it."

"Well, duh, I wasn't planning on wearing it to feed Nana's cats."

"The necklace, Ashley. I was saying your necklace would be safer here in Sacramento when you're at Stanford." Sometimes it was difficult to get her to focus.

"Oh, sure. I'm leaving it here when I go."

"I'll miss you, too, you know," I said as I started kissing her.

"Do you want to come with me tomorrow to feed the cats? Afterward we can hang out."

"Yeah, I've got the early shift tomorrow, but I can pick you up around eleven."

"Perfect!"

Of course, the next day when I showed up at her house at eleven, she was nowhere near ready to go. She was busily texting everybody she knew and then we had to make a stop on the way for cat food. Ashley is beautiful but totally unorganized.

Her grandmother's house on Crocker Road was really impressive. It was big and had a huge yard around it and a wide driveway that went all the way around to the back. There was a pool and, behind that, a smaller house, plus a gazebo on the lawn next to the patio. When Ashley let us in the back door, I noticed the alarm wasn't set. I asked her about it and she said, "Nana never uses it. She said just having the alarm company sign is good enough."

We came through to the kitchen, where we were greeted by a bunch of mewling cats. Ashley threw the cat food onto a counter and started petting them and picking them up one by one for cuddling. She felt compelled to introduce them to me.

"Jason, meet Hiss and Boo. They're sister and brother. And this little tabby is Lilliput. Now these two great big darlings are named Buttons and Bows. And this precious white kitten is Snowball. Isn't she adorable?"

"Huh? Oh, yeah, adorable." I was looking around the room and thinking it would be a lot better with some newer appliances. It wasn't bad, just looked like an old person's kitchen. While Ashley started opening cans, I petted the cats as if I liked them.

Suddenly, Ashley said, "Oh, Jason! Where's Cleopatra? I don't see her anywhere!"

"Who? Another cat?"

"Yes! I don't see her!"

"Maybe she's just off sleeping someplace."

"No, she's always here with the others when I feed them. She's Nana's favorite! Could you go see if you could find her?" She looked worried, but everything with Ashley is a big deal.

"No problem. I'll go find her." After going through the dining room chanting, "Here, Cleopatra. Here, kitty, kitty," I went upstairs. It wasn't hard to figure out which bedroom was Nana's. It was the only one that looked used.

The room was massive and the furniture was antique. I gravitated to the dresser with its collection of mother-of-pearl inlaid jewelry boxes. The first one I opened had a pair of diamond dome earrings easily worth over twenty thousand dollars. I lifted them out and held them up to the light. I picked up the matching dome ring, which could bring in another five grand. As I looked at these things, and thought about how easily I could unload them, I had an epiphany.

This wasn't my break. My big break was Ashley herself! She was spoiled and immature and talked too much, but people could change. Especially when they fall in love. I started imagining our future together. Her parents would make sure I met the right people and got a decent job where I made real money and didn't have to put up with a lot of bull. Eventually, probably in the not too distant future, old Nana would be gone and we'd inherit her stuff and maybe even the house.

"Jason, what are you doing in here?"

I turned to see a frowning Ashley in the doorway, holding a huge gray cat in her arms.

"Sorry, Ashley. I just couldn't resist taking a peek when I saw Nana's jewelry boxes here. Like I told you before, I've always appreciated the skill and artistry that goes into making such exquisite pieces."

"Well, I don't think Nana would like you going through her things." She was still frowning.

"You're right. Don't worry, I just looked at a couple in this box and put them right back like I found them." I walked over to her and leaned down to kiss her forehead. "I'm sorry, babe. Hey, is this the famous Cleopatra I've been searching for?" I gently scratched behind the cat's ears and she started purring.

"Yes, this naughty kitty was hiding. But now she's going to join the others for din-din." Ashley was smiling again.

After the cats were fed, Ashley had me drive her back home. I said I thought we were going to hang out together. She went on and on at lightning speed about how she'd had to reschedule her nail appointment and then her friend Briana had texted her about a fight she'd had with her boyfriend and ... Believe me, she could make a ten-minute drive feel like an hour in a dentist's chair.

The next day I got a panicky text from her. She had some big emergency and needed me to get to her house immediately. When I got there, her dad was on the phone and barely glanced at me when he let me in. He waved toward the stairs and went on talking as he turned his back to me. I went up to Ashley's room and found her throwing stuff around like a crazy person. She was digging through some boxes on her bed and then running in and out of her walk-in closet.

"Ashley," I said, "stop a minute and tell me what's going on."

"Jason, you have to help me! I can't find the necklace Nana gave me."

She was so upset, I had to refrain from pointing out that it would take a miracle to find anything in that mess. "Calm down. I'm here and I'll help you find it. Where did you last see it?"

She fluttered over to her dresser and then handed me a long, thin, jewelry box. "It was in here." She gave me a pathetic look. It was almost as if she thought I could open it and the necklace would be there. Of course, it wasn't.

I started to methodically go through everything looking for it. Ashley kept searching the same drawers over and over again. She was continually stopping to read and return texts, so I was doing most of the work. It was incredible how many clothes she had. I thought again about our future together and smiled.

"Why are you smiling, Jason? Are you making fun of me because I lost my necklace?" She made one of her pouty faces.

"No, not at all. Really, I was just thinking about us."

"Us? And how glad you are to see me go?"

"No way, Ashley." I stopped and took her hands in mine and looked into those vacant blue eyes. "I was just thinking that Palo Alto's not so far away. I can always drive there when I'm not working, and you'll be back here to visit." I grinned and nodded at her phone. "And we'll have texts and Skype."

She pulled her hands free and picked up her phone again as she stepped away. "Well, uh, I was thinking about the future, too, and since I'm going away and this is going to be such a new beginning for me, maybe we should take a break for a while."

The muscles in my jaw tightened as the smile left my face. I couldn't believe this was happening. "So you're breaking up with me?"

"No, I still want us to be friends. I like you. It's just I'll be far away and meeting new people ...."

As though on cue, in walked Zach, her high school jock ex-boyfriend. I knew all about him, having heard from Ashley how he had broken up with her right before graduation. When we started working together, she was on the rebound. I found that to be a good opportunity, if you have the patience to spend hours listening to every boring detail of the breakup, like I did. Zach had been at Cheesecake Factory with us, but I could've sworn he was dating one of the other girls.

"What are you doing here?" I saw no reason to be subtle.

"I thought Ashley might need some help getting packed." He looked at the mess and said to her, "Gee, Ash, you can't take all this." Then he flopped onto her bed.

"OK now, Zach. Don't you start on me," Ashley said. But I could see by the look she gave him that all was well between those two.

Naturally, I wanted to beat his face in. But I settled for spitting out a few well-chosen words at Ashley before I walked out. I muttered a couple of other expletives when I reached the bottom of the stairs, not seeing her mom standing off to the side. I should've apologized, but I was too mad to stop.

As soon as I got home, I grabbed a beer from the fridge and shut myself up in my room. My mom heard the doors slamming and came knocking.

"Not now, Mom."

"Jason? I have to tell you something, son."

"Later, Mom."

She kept talking through the door. "You remember my friend Leann? The one who does horoscopes and psychic readings?"

"Go away, Mom."

She didn't take the hint. "You never called her, but I talked her into doing another reading for you. She said you'll meet the female with the initial 'A' very soon."

"Nice, Mom, but the female has come and gone already."

"No, I'm pretty sure Leann said it's in the future. You still need to be very careful."

"Will do."

"I'm off to Bingo, sweetie. There's a casserole in the fridge. Don't wait up."

"Thanks, Mom." I was already sending a text as I heard her walking away.

There was no way I was stupid enough to go back to Nana's cat farm and take a few family jewels. But I'd kept in touch with a guy who I knew would be perfect for what I had in mind. I'd give him all the information he'd need to get in and out of the old lady's house fast, and I'd be sure to be seen working and occupied somewhere else the whole time. I also sent a couple of texts to some contacts I had in Reno, too, to make sure they were still available to move the jewels.

The next day I went to work as usual. I knew Ashley hadn't been scheduled to work, so I wouldn't have to deal with her. My shift was just about over and I still hadn't heard from my friends when the police walked in. Mike had been thrilled to point me out to them and stood grinning as they led me out. Ashley's necklace was still missing and now Nana's house had been burglarized. I was escorted downtown and booked for crimes I never had the chance to commit.

***

I'd been out on bail, and my hearing date was coming up fast. I got an appointment to talk to my new public defender, since the first guy transferred out somewhere. The new lawyer was a woman not much older than me. I could just tell right away she was an ambitious, professional type. Her heels clicked rhythmically on the tile floor as she marched into the office carrying a thick folder. As she placed it on the desk between us, she quickly introduced herself. She sat and opened the folder and immediately got down to business.

"I've gone over your file, and it looks like the original public defender assigned to your case did a very thorough job."

"Did he tell you that I didn't do it?" I wasn't sure what all was in that folder.

"Pardon me?" She looked slightly startled.

"I didn't steal Ashley's necklace and I didn't steal anything from her grandmother's house either. Like I told the other guy, I was set up."

"The prosecution has a very strong case. You knew about the jewelry, you had access, and your prints were at both Ashley's house and the other house on Crocker Road."

"Because I was dating Ashley." I didn't add that I'd been a little in love with her.

"Yes, and you also had motive. She broke up with you, and witnesses heard you angrily calling her names as you stormed out of her house. Your phone records indicate some incriminating texts sent later that day."

"Yeah, I was mad. And I texted a couple of guys I know. But isn't all of that just circumstantial evidence? I mean, the police practically tore my mom's house apart and never found anything."

"Authorities weren't able to locate the people you texted. However, since the messages weren't answered, they haven't yet pursued it any further." She looked me straight in the eye. "Everyone would like to know where the jewelry is."

I was determined to keep my cool. "Did anybody ask Zach? He was there, too. Did Ashley mention him?"

She sifted through some papers. "Zachary Bennet? Yes, he's one of the witnesses. He's currently sharing an apartment with Ashley, and they returned to Sacramento together to give their depositions."

"Really? They came all the way from Palo Alto?" I wasn't totally surprised that they were together, but I couldn't resist the sarcasm. The lawyer gave me a quizzical frown.

"No, they live in Los Angeles, in Westwood. Ashley is studying drama and Zach is attending UCLA."

"She was going to Stanford ...," I started, but then it hit me. "Where did she get the money? I can't believe her parents would pay for that!"

"Well, the insurance company paid off on the necklace and other jewelry as soon as they received the police report, so Ashley would have something from that. Since it's the company where her mother is executive vice president, it's no surprise the claim settled so quickly."

"So I'm screwed." I slouched back in the chair. "Amazing. Ashley really can act." Then I told my lawyer what I knew, but of course couldn't prove, happened.

She made some notes. "I know the assistant DA on this case and I can talk to him. No promises, but since Ashley's father has just announced his senate run, I believe he'll want to avoid any hint of a family scandal and fraud. We might get a break."

I liked the way she said "we." I realized I hadn't caught her name until she handed me her card. Alicia Azzarello.

R.G. Rose is a Sacramento area writer making her long-awaited publishing debut with *Gimme a Break.* She's currently working on a murder mystery series set in England.

THE GOOD GARDENER

LINDA TOWNSDIN

She dropped her briefcase on the kitchen counter, glanced out the sliding door to the terraced backyard, and gasped. Her jaw slack, Gwen stared at the silk tree stretched diagonally across the yard, branches flaring in all directions, jagged yellow spikes of ripped wood at its broken base.

She flew down the steps into the yard, her low-heeled pumps sinking into the saturated ground. The tree had landed directly onto the raised flower bed of what her husband called her "exotics," smashing them into the rain-soaked soil.

The fern-leafed branches of the *Albizia julibrissin,* common name mimosa or silk tree, had shaded the back section of the property for twenty years, a welcome relief from the Sacramento sun. She'd watered it, pruned it, and raked up leaves and pink pincushion flowers. All that effort and now it was flat on the ground, a useless carcass. She half-cried, half-snorted. She might as well be describing herself.

She hurried back to the house, grabbed her trowel, gloves, and a garbage bag, and sped back to her garden. Dropping to her knees, she wrenched the tree's branches aside and surveyed the damage.

Her flowers were nearly all gone. She fought the tree branches, stuffing what she could reach of her plants into the bag, wiping away angry tears that left streaks of dirt on her cheeks.

She heard the front door slam and looked at her watch. It was four o'clock.

"Mom, you here?" Jason appeared on the deck, his head cocked. "Whoa, did the rain do that to the tree? Is that why you're home so early? Is there anything to eat?"

She turned back to her work. "Check the refrigerator."

"OK. I gotta meet Mike. Be back for dinner."

The door slammed again and he was gone. Seventeen, and he, too, was slipping through her fingers, just as Shelley had when she left for her new job at the Capitol. The nonprofit Gwen worked for was only a few blocks away in one of the many nondescript concrete state buildings, but Shelley was always too busy for lunch.

Gwen used to worry that her biggest fault as a mother was that she did too much for her children. All the books said if you did things for them they could do themselves, they would have difficulty functioning in the world as responsible adults. Not so in Shelley's case. Her daughter thrived on her own. She even sounded slightly impatient the last few times Gwen called to see if she needed anything. Her son would be fine on his own too, once he figured out that food didn't magically appear at mealtime.

When they were younger she spent so much time with her children—birthday and Halloween parties in her carefully tended backyard, barbecues with the neighbors and their kids, all under the silk tree's canopy. She stabbed the trowel into the ground and continued hacking at the once vibrant, red, violet, and white flowers, now a muddy brown slime.

She counted on her work to fill that empty space when her children were both in school, putting her whole heart into the state-funded organization Science for Kids. She volunteered for everything that needed to be done and never complained at the overtime hours. Madeline, her previous marketing VP, said she couldn't get along without Gwen.

Madeline left for a job in the Bay Area last year, but instead of promoting Gwen, they hired Howard Branson, who was half her age and half her height. He reminded her of one of those egg-shaped toy people her kids used to play with, weighted at the bottom so they wobbled but never toppled. Branson never said, "I've asked Gwen to handle that project." He said, "I've *tasked* Gwen."

She'd been a good mother and a good employee. She sat back on her heels and looked at her yard. And a good gardener. Where had it gotten her? Her cell phone rang. Jean's name came up, her loud friend from work. She turned off the ringer, wanting nothing more than to blot out the day. "It wasn't supposed to happen like this." She yanked up a root.

***

Someone shook her arm. "Hon, what are you doing?" Her husband's broad face looked down at her.

Her voice trembled, tears pooled at the corners of her eyes. She wanted to tell him what happened, but all she could say was, "Yesterday's storm blew down the silk tree."

He put a hand on her shoulder. "I see that. And a shame it wrecked your exotics, but please try not to take it so hard."

"Don't you get it, everything I've worked for is ruined!" She rammed more smashed plants into her bag.

He said, "Look at you. You've stained your suit. C'mon, let's go in the house and have tea. We'll get someone out to clean this up."

He took her elbow and helped her up, brushing dirt from her jacket. A sticky mass the color of dried blood stuck to her shoe. Tom said, "I always liked those red flowers." He reached for the garbage bag but she pushed his hand away. "I'm already filthy. I'll take it."

She threw the bag into a bin at the side of the house and tossed her gloves and shoes in with it.

Inside, she called to Tom. "I'm taking a shower." In the bathroom, she dropped her suit and blouse into the trash and stood under scalding hot water, scrubbing her skin raw.

Crawling into bed, she said, "I'm exhausted. Can you put a frozen pizza in the oven?"

Tom's eyes widened. "Are you sick? It's not like you to leave work early. I'll call Dr. Huang."

She reached out a hand. Tom would know how to fix it. Her voice shook slightly. "I have to tell you something."

He stood over her, his voice gentle. "What is it? You know you can tell me anything."

The words wouldn't form. Instead, she said, "Don't call the doctor. I'm just sad about my yard."

At six o'clock, Jason walked past her room, talking low into his phone. "I swear, Shelley, Mom's acting weird. She came home from work and went crazy because of that tree falling and then she started digging in her garden in her work clothes."

He came in the room and handed Gwen the phone. "Shelley wants to say hi."

"Mom? Jase said you're really upset. I'm so sorry, but I'll help you replant."

Gwen could picture her daughter's eyebrows drawn together with concern. Shelley was tall and slender, her straight brown hair hanging in waves around her perfectly oval face. People said they looked alike, but when they had photos taken together, Gwen's features appeared out of focus. Her daughter always faced the camera straight on, one hand on her hip. Gwen angled away, hands folded in front of her, head tilted down, her hair falling forward like a veil across her cheek.

Shelley said, "I have to go. I'm on deadline on a project for the senator. Are you sure you're OK?"

"I'm fine. Don't worry about it."

Tom brought her dinner on a tray and handed her cell phone to her. "You left it in the kitchen. Looks like a couple messages from Jean."

She glanced at the bubbles of text. One said, "I'm so sorry!" The other said, "Call me!"

Gwen turned the phone off and pushed the tray away. "The soup looks great, but I can't eat right now."

Tom patted the mound of her leg under the blanket. "You'll be fine after a good night's rest. You've been putting in too many hours at that job."

Gwen knew her husband expected her to snap out of it, not because he was insensitive, but because that was her history. Whatever the obstacle, she soldiered on. She'd always been steadfast. Some people might consider it a boring attribute, but she felt pride in the trait, which made her an asset to Science for Kids. She knew that department better than anyone, and yet they'd brought in the Weeble to run it.

***

The next morning Jason left for school and Tom was leaving for Modesto. A lobbyist, he traveled throughout the state most weekdays. He gently shook her arm until her eyes opened. She glanced at the clock—seven thirty. She'd slept all evening and through the night.

She croaked, "I dreamed a violent wind knocked me down, and each time I tried to get up it blew me down again."

He said, "You'll feel better if you go in to work."

She cleared her throat. "Maybe in a while."

He started to say something else, but must have thought better of it. He nodded and said, "They're coming to remove the tree this morning."

After Tom left, Gwen got up to go to the bathroom, but her heart pounded so hard she thought she was having a heart attack. She clung to the wall on her way back to bed. She'd wanted to talk to him; he was her best friend. Only she'd never had anything like this to tell him before.

Gwen was proud to work for a nonprofit that promoted science programs in schools. She'd won the Most Valuable Employee award last year before Branson arrived. They gave her an eagle's head on a wooden base, her name etched into a gold plaque on the front. They counted on her and she always came through. They'd said she was too valuable in her current job to promote her to manager of the marketing department.

When she'd talked to the marketing VP about expecting a promotion, he said, "You're the only one who knows your system. We'd be lost without you coordinating everything. We thought you'd be pleased with the raise."

Maybe she'd been too careful protecting her turf, never sharing her procedures or information about where she kept important files. She thought her secrets were her power.

When Branson came on board, he wasted no time. He gathered her team in a conference room and drew charts outlining his vision for programs and projects that covered the whiteboard as high as he could reach. He scheduled weekly brainstorming sessions, and bobbed up and down brandishing his marker like a saber.

Gwen dutifully prepared the budgets and timelines for his projects, but delays, cost overruns, and lost materials plagued each step until Branson put them on hold. The aborted projects left the team confused and exhausted. Behind his back, Gwen's team called him Back Burner Branson. Eventually, the team fell apart. Several transferred to other departments. One left the organization. No one knew if it was voluntary.

Loud buzzing from the back of the house meant the tree people had arrived. Gwen dressed and stood at the patio door watching the workers chop off the limbs and drag them away. They dug up the stump and filled in the hole. You would never know the tree had ever been there, except for a few scraped places in the grass. She moved to the kitchen window at the front of the house and watched as they shoved the branches into a chipper.

When the truck was gone, she put on her garden shoes, gathered gloves and trowel, took a deep breath, and headed out to remove what remained of her mangled flowers now that the tree no longer obstructed access.

She yanked them up, hurled them into the garbage bag, and turned the ground with fierce determination until nothing remained but smooth brown soil.

A transplanted Easterner, she'd known nothing about Sacramento trees and plants that grew all year long. But she'd gradually become an expert in all kinds of exotic plants and flowers. Maybe she'd neglected the silk tree, paying more attention to the flowers. It had to have been rotting for months.

***

Tom came home at five thirty. Gwen was back in bed. He scratched his head. "You didn't go to work?"

She forced herself to speak. "Don't worry about it. I've accrued more than five hundred hours of unused sick leave. Working in the yard wore me out, that's all."

"I'm really sorry you lost all your favorite plants. You can replant, can't you?"

Her smile felt more like a grimace. "Maybe someday." She'd never replant, no matter how many people suggested it.

She heard Tom answer the doorbell when it rang that evening. It sounded like Jean. She could hear them as they walked through the quiet house toward the bedroom.

"I feel terrible for Gwen," said Jean. "How's she taking it?"

"Nothing's ever upset her like this before. I figured a day or two and she'd be OK."

"You did? This was a major blow! People can get really depressed when it happens."

"Come on, Jean, this is not the end of the world."

"Tom! I'm shocked at your attitude. To be let go with no warning and—"

"What did you say?"

Jean's voice rose. "Gwen didn't tell you they fired her? The rumor is mismanagement of funds. Branson said she sabotaged his department. Our Gwen! No way."

"A tree blew down and she … I didn't know."

"What does that have to do with anything?"

"She said she was upset about losing the tree and her favorite plants were destroyed. She didn't tell us she'd lost her job."

Their voices dropped to a whisper and Tom came into the bedroom, a dazed look on his face. "Jean's here to see you."

Jean's red head peeked around the doorframe, followed by her angular body. "This was totally unfair. No one believes it was your fault. I just wanted to say how sorry I am."

Gwen's eyes slid from Jean's face. "I can't talk about it."

"I understand. Promise me you'll call me soon, OK?"

Gwen sent a look to Tom—the one they used at parties when one of them wanted to be rescued from a conversation. He took

Jean's elbow and led her out. "She'll call you in a couple of days."

He came back in a few minutes and sat down heavily on the bed. "Will you please tell me what happened?"

Her voice wavered. "You heard. Branson fired me."

"I felt like a jerk talking to Jean about a tree." Tom stared at her as if she were a stranger. "Why didn't you tell me?"

She looked at her hands. "I couldn't believe it myself."

Brows furrowed, he said, "Mismanaging funds? You've never mismanaged anything in your life." He laid back against his pillow and rolled next to her. She let him tip her on her side and move into their spoon position, his soft bulk pillowing around her thin bones. Angry tears made diagonal paths across her cheek. She punched the pillow. "That twerp Branson actually stood over me while I cleaned out my desk—slurping his ever-present green smoothie. He walked me out the door like I was a criminal."

It had been satisfying over the past year to watch Branson's face turn red as he bobbed and weaved on his tiny feet, making excuses to the marketing VP about why his projects were never ready to roll out. She'd racked up the cost overruns by missing deadlines, making it look like Branson's indecision was the problem. She'd hidden work that had to be redone, suggesting he'd misplaced it, and planted rumors that he was unreliable. Her lips twisted. He'd complained the strain was giving him an ulcer.

Tom said, "Maybe we should get away for a while, take a vacation as soon as I get back from L.A. next week. How does that sound?"

"Do you really see me frolicking on a beach right now?"

Their landline rang. Tom squinted at the caller ID. "What's Jean calling for now?"

Gwen's gut clenched. "Don't answer it."

He picked up the phone. "What's up, Jean? It's late."

He listened, said, "My God," hung up, and turned to Gwen, his eyes boring into her. "Branson died an hour ago. Some gastric thing."

She expelled a deep breath and hid her face in the pillow, not sure if she could control her expression. "That's terrible, Tom. I didn't know he was ill." Another lie. She'd been poisoning his smoothies for weeks with doses of her deadly nicotiana plant, the attractive one with fuchsia flowers that Tom thought were so pretty.

When a loyal coworker told Gwen she was going to be let go, she'd gone into her garden that night, picked a much larger quantity, ground it up, and stirred it into his green smoothie in the morning. He always stored it in the break room refrigerator. She watched him gulp it down while he fired her, a dribble of green hanging from his lower lip. She hadn't planned to kill him, just make him suffer.

Tom sat next to Gwen on the bed, looking dazed. "We have to put all this behind us."

She raised her head, a spark of hope blossoming in her chest. Tom was right. She didn't need to dwell on the past. She clutched his hand. "They could hire me back."

Tom said, "I think you should take a break, spend time with the kids, replant your garden." He looked away. "Although maybe not the red flowers."

Linda Townsdin writes the *Spirit Lake Mystery* series set in Minnesota's lake country. After covering war and disaster worldwide, Britt Johansson, a freelance photojournalist with a big heart and bit of an attitude returns to her Spirit Lake home to recharge—where something bad always happens. *Focused on Murder* (2014), *Close Up on Murder (2015), Blow Up on Murder (2016).* Lindatownsdin.com.

CHRISTMAS CHRONICLES

DANNA WILBERG

Ruby Leham propped herself against the edge of the kitchen table. "Beth didn't come home last night," she said, twisting life from her daughter's favorite sweater. *Three days 'til Christmas. How could she?*

Ed Leham peered over the morning sports page, sipping his coffee. "Whadidja expect? She's a damn alley cat. How many times have we scoured Sacramento looking for her? Ten? Twenty? Last time she showed up after five weeks, hungry— and *pregnant*! Please don't ask me to go through that again, Rubes. I'm done. Finito! She wants to ruin her life, so be it."

Ruby held back tears. Ed was right. Their daughter decided long ago rules didn't apply to her. *Been a handful for sixteen years.* When Beth came home pregnant, Ruby hoped a baby would change their daughter's behavior. Within a week, Beth acquired a new boyfriend and a *flat stomach*. Nothing slowed the girl down. *Nothing.*

***

One block over, Shamus Doyle burst through the door. Hysteria strangled his vocal chords into a screech. "Jesus H. Christ! Call the cops! Someone stole my freakin' car!"

His wife, Natalie, rose from the couch, cuddling their infant daughter to her breast. "Calm down, Shamus. You'll scare the baby." Shamus tugged at his hair, a habit he developed after his second tour in Iraq. His jerky movements alerted Natalie shit was about to hit the fan. Her heart sank. Shamus had finally landed a job at Folsom Outlet Stores. *Hired for the holiday rush.* They were a one-car family. Natalie shuddered, afraid to ask, "How will you get to work?"

***

At 6:45 a.m., twelve-year-old Tommy Pitts rode his bike past his neighbors. *Odd.* Shamus Doyle's precious midnight-blue beamer wasn't parked in its usual space, yet Tommy heard Doyle and his wife yelling inside the house. Tommy hated when they fought. *Can't worry about it now. Got troubles of my own.* His cat, Shall, short for "He Shall Not Be Named," had gone missing the night before. Shall, black with one taffy-colored paw, had adopted a routine Tommy could set his watch by: dinner at six, followed by two hours of hunting, stalking, and spraying the Doyles' fence. Tommy opened the door promptly at eight, at which time the cat would come inside, curl in front of the TV, and settle in for the night. When Shall didn't show up, Tommy scoured the backyard. Shall was nowhere to be found.

Tommy rode down P Street, sped across 7th, avoided a near-miss with a motorist, and circled the block once more. The weather had turned cold. Shall probably had taken refuge nearby. *Maybe someone stole him. Maybe ...* Tommy pushed away images of stiff fur, empty eye-sockets crawling with maggots.

***

At 7:00 a.m. sharp, Janey Fry slid behind her desk, pressed the power button on her computer, and waited for her monitor to spring to life. When the familiar *bing* sounded, she typed FACEBOOK in her browser and hit enter. Once the site loaded, she began to type:

SOME ASSHOLE IN A DARK BLUE B-MER NEARLY RAN ME OVER ON P STREET LAST NIGHT! WHY CAN'T PEOPLE SLOW DOWN? LUCKILY, I GOT OUT OF HIS WAY IN TIME. OTHERWISE, YOU WOULD BE READING MY OBITUARY TODAY!

Janey added a photo of a smashed bug to her entry and pressed 'Post.' Within minutes, she received twenty-two 'Likes' and one comment:

Priscilla B. Did you catch the douche bag's license plate number? I'd call the police and report the jerk before someone gets seriously killed.

Janey F. @PB, good idea! Caught last 3 digits -008 ☺ Calling SPD!

Janey called the Sacramento Police Department and reported the incident. "Unfortunately," the dispatcher said, "without a complete plate number it would be hard to locate the driver. You're welcome to come down to the station and file a complaint." *Blah, blah, blah.* Janey opened her browser to Yahoo and scanned the news. Her job included researching fun facts for the deejays to spin into drama at radio station NOW 100.5. Instead, she clicked on a link headlined Woman's Body Found in Calaveras County. "Thank God it's not Sacramento," she said.

***

Sacramento P.D. dispatcher Adam Fitch clocked in at 7:01 a.m., still rattled by the kid who flew across 7th and P Street on his bike, nearly becoming a hood ornament. Fitch wanted a drink. A drink and a place to pound on something. He wanted to turn back time and kiss the face manifesting behind his bloodshot eyes. Bittersweet memories ensued: tiny pearl earrings, *thank you, Daddy*. Corrin's fifteenth birthday, *the day she disappeared*. He seethed over kids who lived life recklessly. He would give the world to hold his only child again.

His painful moment proved equally short-lived when the phone rang and Shamus Doyle screamed into his ear, "I want to report a stolen BMW!" Two minutes later, a woman sobbed into the phone, "My daughter didn't come home last night." Adam reached for the 'special' coffee creamer hidden on the far right side of his desk drawer. He poured two fingers into his Star Wars cup and drank it down. The liquid burned in his throat, the fire in his belly raged. *Another missing girl.*

***

Rex Reynolds sucked at games old men play, like cribbage and pinochle. His forte? Convincing children he was a decent human being in need of their help. His pitch involved lost dogs, cats, or simply being lost himself. No one would suspect the frail-looking man to be blessed with his strength, or to handle a knife with his skill. Rex prided himself on being a monster. *Twenty years in prison.* He learned a lot. He was an expert locksmith, mechanic, and psychologist. Sometimes he pretended to be homeless. *Harmless.* Like a spider, he spun his web and waited for his victims.

Rex pulled into his garage on T Street and turned off the motor. His 1963 Pontiac resided temporarily at his friend Steve's house on the next block. Rex traded Steve, a "body" man, a generator rebuild on a 1978 Javelin for a paint job on his Bonneville. Any other day, you wouldn't catch Rex driving a BMW. "Deathtraps" is what he and his buddy Steve would call any car built after 1980. However, this BMW was special ... A sweet surprise laid waiting inside the trunk.

First things first. Rex retrieved a bulging pillowcase from the back seat of the car. The squirming animal inside growled and spit.

"Oh, c'mon now. I didn't hurt you." Rex unlocked the side door to the garage, untied the twine holding the pillowcase closed, but held the opening tight until he stepped outdoors. He bent low to the ground and released the cat. The cat scurried to the edge of his lawn, stretched, and licked one taffy-colored paw. Rex hissed and stamped his foot. The cat no longer served a purpose. "Go! Go home!" When the cat took off, Rex returned to his garage. *Gettin' late.* He had *things to do.*

***

At 7:05 a.m., Adam Fitch dispatched an investigation team to the Leham residence. An Amber Alert was issued at 7:30 a.m. The missing girl's description hit the airwaves at 7:31. Height, five-foot-two; red, curly hair; green eyes. Date of birth, June 14, 2000. Same year his daughter was born. Beth Leham was *six months older.* His heart thrummed an extra beat. The

Lehams saw their daughter yesterday. *Corrin went missing five years ago.*

***

At 7:32 Rex donned a half mask resembling a wolf, and popped the trunk latch. A smile parted his thick lips. "Hi there, pretty girl. Ready for a little fun?" The girl's squint grew into wide-eyed fear. Although duct tape prevented a scream from escaping her mouth, her groan was substantial as she recoiled from his touch. Rex watched her small frame buck and twist against the restraints. *Feisty.* He liked them that way. Breaking their spirit added to his excitement.

He tossed the now-empty pillowcase at the teen's feet and lifted a red tendril from her wet cheek. "Don't cry. I ain't gonna hurt you none." Laughter welled in his chest and bubbled upward until his shoulders shook. "You *are* precious," he said, pressing a chloroformed rag over her nose. Her eyes fluttered and closed. Her body went limp. Rex hoisted the girl over his shoulder, but on the way to his lair, the doorbell rang. He waited. Listened. *Walkie-talkies?* Ringing segued to door pounding. In haste, he returned the girl to the trunk and removed his mask.

Rex opened the front door slowly, rubbing his eyes. Two uniformed officers appeared stone-faced on his doorstep.

"Rex Reynolds? I'm Officer Sparks, this is Officer Larson."

"Yes. Can I help y—" Rex broke into a phlegmy cough. He yanked a rag from his pocket and deposited the wet glob gurgling in his throat. Chloroform fumes tickled his nostrils.

"We're combing the neighborhood for a young girl who went missing last night."

Rex wheezed, and continued his coughing fit. The officers turned to each other, exchanging a glance. The older officer spoke up. "Where were you last night, Mr. Reynolds?"

"Home. In bed." Rex doubled over with a tenacious bark.

The young officer took a step backward. He pulled a business card from his pocket, placed it between two fingers,

181

and handed it to Rex. "If you think of anything, give this number a call. Understand?"

Rex nodded, exploding into another round of whooping. He held his chest for effect.

"Take care of that cough, Mr. Reynolds. Good day."

Once the officers turned to go, Rex shut the door. This time, the wheeze blossomed into laughter. *Dumbshits*. He peeked out the window. The officers split up and circled his house. *Uh oh.* Maybe they weren't so dumb, after all. Rex watched through slatted blinds until the officers rejoined forces on the sidewalk. His heart progressed from trot to gallop when the younger officer bent down and picked up the black cat with one taffy-colored paw. The older officer examined the tag on the cat's collar. *Next time get a damn dog*, Rex noted to himself. Just then, a young boy skidded his bicycle to a halt. "Shall!" Rex heard the boy shout. Soon, the officers and the boy were smiling and laughing. "Go do your happy dance somewhere else," Rex seethed. He had a party of his own to get started.

As if all four, including the cat, could read his mind, they all turned in his direction. Chills skittered up Rex's spine. The boy gathered his bike and cat and nodded goodbye. The officers lingered another minute or two. When they finally got into their squad car and drove away, Rex had the feeling they'd be back. He couldn't take that chance.

***

Before today, Shamus Doyle wouldn't have been caught dead riding public transportation. *Two shopping days left before Christmas.* If he wanted to keep his job, he needed to get to work. He checked his watch. Light rail arrived in Folsom before the stores opened. *An hour late is better than not showing up at all.* His new boss seemed to understand his predicament, but skipping the gym that morning made Shamus anxious. *Exercise produces endorphins.* He needed all the help he could get. He felt like a ticking time bomb.

***

Once the police gave up snooping around his house, Rex decided his little red-headed treasure wasn't worth another twenty-five to life. "Don't have twenty-five years left in my bucket." On his way to the garage, he stopped in the bathroom to take a leak. "Be lucky if I have ten," he mumbled. Time sure had crept up on him.

He took a risk dumping the vehicle in broad daylight, but better to get rid of it now than take a chance on the police returning with a warrant. He replaced the license plate on the BMW with one he had pilfered a few years back. The vehicle tag appeared to be up-to-date. "Yep, learned all kinds of tricks in the joint."

Rex slipped behind the wheel and headed for the highway.

***

Adam realized how important the first twenty-four hours were to a missing person case. All available officers had been dispatched to canvass the area near the Lehams' home. In many instances, victims were abducted within five miles of their home. Jaycee Dugard came to mind. Adam's heart picked up its pace. Acid churned in his gut. The thought of any little girl ending up like Jaycee Dugard made him want to vomit. *Let's hope Beth Leham is found unharmed. Soon.*

Adam poured over the sex offender list frozen on his computer screen. *They're everywhere*. He pushed back in his chair and laced his hands behind his head. He closed his eyes and imagined his daughter, Corrin, sitting at the piano, her face intent on mastering her craft. When his heart regained a normal beat, he leaned forward and went over the list once more.

***

Shamus stood on the platform at 7th and Capitol Mall. When the train arrived, he hurried inside, clambering for the last seat against the wall. The car filled to two-thirds of its capacity in seconds. Shamus opened his jacket, loosened his tie, and inhaled deeply. Once his lungs filled with air, he exhaled. He repeated this exercise until his hands stopped shaking and the ringing in his ears subsided. He had a wife and new baby to think of. This job meant putting food on the table, paying the rent. He couldn't afford to blow it, but *damn*, didn't he have the crummiest luck?

The train arrived in Folsom on time. A quick walk across the parking lot and he'd be at work.

***

Rex exited Highway 50 at Folsom Boulevard. He planned to dump the car in the Folsom Outlet parking lot and catch the light rail home. *Easy, peasy.* He scoped out the perfect spot. A cluster of parked cars close to the walkway leading to the train caught his eye. *Employees?* Stores didn't open until nine. He circled four rows closest to the street, settling on a vacancy between a Volkswagen and a Toyota. He had exactly seven minutes to get to the platform to catch the next train.

With five minutes to spare, Rex inserted two one-dollar bills into the kiosk and retrieved his ticket from the metal slot. When the train arrived, he waited for passengers to disembark before boarding the train. He moved toward the back of the car and slid into the seat against the wall.

***

Inside the trunk of the car, Beth regained consciousness. She heard muffled sounds. Car doors opening. Car doors closing. *Voices.* She pulled her knees to her chest and kicked the underside of the trunk with all her might. *Boom.* Again. *Boom.* Again. *Boom.* Nothing. She whimpered, and cried. She groaned in frustration. She kicked every surface her feet made contact with inside the confined space until finally, *someone heard.*

Out of habit, Shamus wound his way through the section of parking lot occupied by Folsom Outlet employees. When he heard a thump, he glanced to his right. His jaw dropped. He couldn't believe his eyes. Had he manifested his BMW by merely wishing it so? As he drew near, his jubilation waned. *Not my license plate.* His inner voice intervened. *What about the rims?* He'd know those rims anywhere. Each Saturday, he'd detail every nook and cranny until they gleamed. He needed a closer look. When he approached the car, he heard it again. Louder this time. *The trunk?* He tapped on the shiny surface. The voice was strained. The terror? Clear as a bell. Shamus reached in his pocket and extracted his keys. "Please don't let this be a dream," he said unlocking the trunk. The girl inside shook with relief.

***

Tears formed in Adam's eyes when he got the call. Shamus Doyle reported that not only had he found his beloved BMW, the contents needed immediate attention. *Beth Leham, alive and well.* Once Adam dispatched a call to Folsom PD and emergency services, he reached in his drawer for a celebratory toast. He was about to take a drink when Elaine Jordan slapped a memo on his desk. "Here, this came in earlier. The woman claims she was almost struck by a vehicle last night. The driver didn't stop. She didn't have more than the description of the car and last three numbers of the plate. I noticed the car matches a description on the grand theft auto list." With that said, Elaine stifled a yawn and added, "What wrong? You coming down with the flu or something? Your face is flushed."

Adam drummed his fingers on the piece of paper. "Wow," was all he could say. "Wow, wow, wow." He shuffled through the stack of papers on his desk until he found what he was looking for—Shamus Doyle's stolen car report. His finger trailed down the page. License plate number NCC12008. "I'll be damned. We have a match."

***

"Are all these questions necessary? She's been through enough," Ruby Leham told Officer Sparks. "She needs her rest."

"We apologize, Mrs. Leham, but there's still a kidnapper out there. We need to document what Beth remembers."

"It's OK, Mom." Beth patted her mother's hand. She turned to her father and said, "Daddy, why don't you take mom for a cup of coffee? I'll be fine."

Sparks eased toward the door, inviting the Lehams to depart.

Ed and Ruby exchanged glances. Ruby surmised Ed would be happier anywhere than in this room. Her shenanigans had scrubbed him clean of any emotion. "Fine, you have my permission. But we won't be long," she said.

Beth sat up in bed, drew her legs to her chest, and wrapped her arms around her knees. "I peed myself I was so scared."

"I can only imagine," Sparks said, his voice gentle as rain. "Where did you first see the person who took you?"

"I was on my way home. About a block from my house, I saw this old man. He—he was looking for his cat. It was cold, dark. I offered to help. Next thing I know—I woke up in the trunk of a car."

"Tell me about the old man. What did he look like?"

"I don't know. Old."

"How old?"

"Older than my Grandpa, who passed away two years ago."

Larson stepped forward. "What did he say to you?"

"Nothing. He was calling his cat. I felt sorry for him. I thought I saw something under the bushes. Even though the cat was black, it had one paw that was different. Kinda light brown or something."

"What happened after that?"

"I got the cat, gave it to him, and he thanked me."

"Then what?"

"I started walking home."

Officer Sparks noted her testimony on his pad and met her gaze. "Do you remember what happened next?"

Her focus shifted toward the ceiling. "I was tied up. He wore a mask. A wolf. I could see his eyes, looking at me, like I was dinner." Tears streamed down her face. "He said I was pretty. Why did that make me feel good?"

Sparks sat on the edge of the bed and took Beth's hand. "You must've been relieved when he opened the trunk. Being locked away in the dark with little oxygen can be scary."

"Yeah, I suppose you're right."

"What about his voice?" Larson interjected. "Did it sound familiar?"

"Yes and no. At first I thought—"

"Thought what, Beth?" Sparks leaned in.

"Well, he kinda sounded like the old man, but not so old. Does that make sense?"

"Did he have a wheeze or a cough?" Larson's voice rose a notch. "Did you smell any odors?"

"Come to think of it, his voice was raspy. I smelled cigarettes. Chemicals."

Sparks rose from the bed. "What else can you tell me about the cat?"

***

Adam Fitch passed the evidence bay on his way to clock out. He saw the forensic team hovering over a pillowcase speckled with tiny flags. "Cat hairs," he heard one of them say. "Black and tan." Adam shook his head. What a weird day. He was glad it was over.

***

When the Lehams returned from their coffee break, Officer Sparks assured them Sacramento Police would keep them abreast of any further development. After bidding them goodbye, Sparks made haste. Hank Larson followed in his wake. "Are you thinking what I'm thinking?"

"Yep!"

"What are the odds the cat we saw outside Reynolds' place is the cat she's talking about?"

"This could be our lucky day!"

"All we need is a warrant."

***

At 7:01 p.m., Officer Sparks and Officer Larson pounded on Rex Reynolds' door, search warrant in hand.

Rex acted shocked, insulted, when they barged into his home, and began going through his things. He spied them examining the wolf mask sitting on the kitchen counter beside the morning mail. "Left over from Halloween," he muttered. "I like dressing up for the kids."

"I'll bet you do," Sparks replied, his tone brimming with sarcasm.

Larson moved across the room. "Where does this door lead to?"

"The basement. Nothin' down there but some old junk from my previous roommate. Skipped on the rent, the son-of-a ... Mind tellin' me what this is all about?"

Larson flipped the light switch and eased through the door with caution. Weapon drawn, he began his descent. He stopped midway and shuddered. The last time he saw anything this horrific was when he visited a torture museum in Germany. He moved closer to the chains and manacles hanging from the rafters. A wooden stool, perched on two legs, rested against one padded wall. Catching a tiny glint with his flashlight beam between the wall and the foundation, he bent down to investigate. Repulsion hit hard when he saw a tiny pearl earring with a bent post.

Rex Reynolds didn't put up a fight when Larson put him in handcuffs. *Three squares a day*, he thought, and a prison dentist to check the molar that'd been giving him fits for the last six months. *Maybe I'll take a yoga class.*

***

Tommy Pitts decided he wanted to be a cop after police came to his home and questioned him about his cat's whereabouts the night of Beth Leham's kidnapping. The officers commended Tommy on his diligence in finding Shall, and told him he and Shall were in part responsible for "cracking the case."

***

Shamus Doyle resorted to riding the train to work until the forensic team finished collecting evidence from his BMW. Grateful for the car's return, he didn't complain. Due to the nature of the crime, and his part in the girl's rescue, Shamus was offered counseling for his PTSD at no cost to him. He agreed seeing a therapist would be helpful.

Janey Fry's post went viral on Facebook when she wrote the following:

News flash! The car that almost ran me over before Christmas turned out to be not only stolen, but driven by a serial killer who had his latest victim stashed in the trunk! :{

***

Beth Leham cleaned her room, erased her contact list from her phone, and stuck close to home. The baby conceived December twenty-second continued to grow in her womb. And although she grimaced every time she thought of Rex Reynolds, a precautionary rape kit taken at the hospital concluded the DNA residue didn't belong to him. Beth knew in her heart he wasn't a match. *Neither was the donor.* Yet, there was something special about *this* baby. *Life is precious.*

Ruby Leham resurrected her crocheting skills. Ed Leham joined a bowling team.

***

Adam Fitch bawled like a baby when he received news his daughter's killer had been found. The nightmare that had begun three days before Christmas ended well for some. Not for him. DNA testing confirmed the pearl earring found in Rex Reynolds' basement belonged to his daughter, Corrin.

Danna Wilberg visits the dark side of human nature through adventure and trepidation in her suspense novels and short stories. Pairing fact with fiction, she delivers an uneasy feeling of possibility that makes one shift in their seat. More on Danna Wilberg novels at www.dannawilberg.com.

More Great Titles from Capitol Crimes

www.KathleenLAsay.com

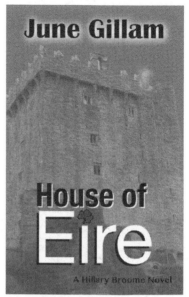

www.Junegillam.com

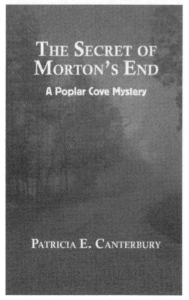

www.patmyst.com

www.mindcandymysteries.
com

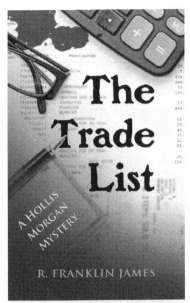

www.rfranklinjames.com

www.patricialmorin.com

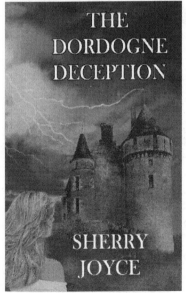

www.sherryjoyce.com

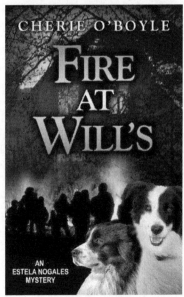

www.cherieoboyle.com

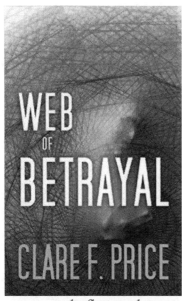

www.webofbetrayal.com

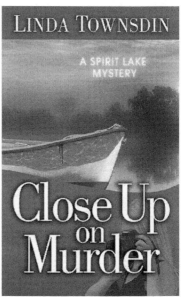

Lindatownsdin.com

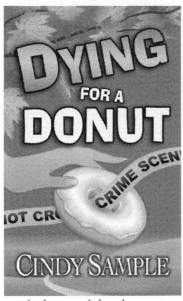

cindysamplebooks.com

https://victorianscribbles.bl
ogspot.com

www.micheleweiss.com

lindawestphal.com

Made in the USA
San Bernardino, CA
24 October 2016